Desol

(The Commorancy — Book 5)

Al K. Line

Alkline.co.uk

Sign up for The Newsletter for news of the latest releases as well as flash sales at Alkline.co.uk

Commorancy: *a dwelling place or ordinary residence of a person. This residence is usually temporary and it is vacated after a given time.*

Feeding Time

"Stop feeding them, what's the point? It's just a waste." Artek's mother stared at him sternly, her immaculate shoe tap, tap, tapping impatiently as she frowned, arms crossed in her usual disappointed way.

"Mother," lectured Artek, "until it is decided whether they are suitable for rule or not then they do need feeding you know? We can't have my reign starting with a bunch of semi-starved subjects, now can we? What kind of an example does that set for the people? Well I'll tell you, not a very good one. Here you go." Artek pushed a tray of food through the bars and the tiny man inside grabbed for it mutely.

His mother walked regally up beside him. "What do we say?" The man just stared at her with uncomprehending eyes, darting from her to Artek, then back to his plate of food, obviously wanting to eat more than anything else. "See? He's a savage. And small. You shouldn't encourage them, it's pointless."

"Eat, take sustenance," said Artek, pointing to the tray and turning his back on the men in the cell, the last one to be given food backing away now attention was no longer on him. Artek grabbed his mother politely by the arm and said, "Shall we walk Mother?"

"Fine, but don't think that I approve of your misplaced sympathy. You need to be ruthless if you are to build our kingdom correctly."

Artek turned and looked at his mother. "You said 'our' Mother, don't you mean 'my' kingdom?"

"Of course I do, my dear, sweet son. But I shall be there with you. I shall be right by your side, helping my boy in any way that I possibly can."

"Most gracious."

~~~

The small man in the cell backed into a corner and huddled close to the others then began to eat his meager meal. All that could be heard were the sounds of food being greedily consumed, the clattering of the metal trays and the bickering of Artek and Malessa Ligertwood, receding into the distance as they made their way down the rows, inspecting the inmates, arguing over their future, or lack of it.

The men paid it no mind, they were in Artek's thrall, unaware that they were captive, just obedient and quiet, somehow knowing that their lives depended on it.

Friendships End

"Well, that's the end of that," said Malessa, standing beside her son in The Communications Room.

"I guess so, for now." Artek smiled, pleased with the way he'd handled talking to Letje.

"Yes, for now. You did well my son, Arcene has been truly invaluable in allowing you to gain access to their systems. It made everything so much easier."

Artek leaned back and sighed.

"What? Are you not pleased?"

"Yes Mother, I am pleased. But I do hope she will be alright. She is to be mine after all."

"Oh, don't worry, I'm sure our little Princess won't get into too much trouble. She is still a child; she will be forgiven. You'll see, witness it for yourself soon enough. I would imagine that it won't be too long before we all meet, won't that be nice?"

A smile spread across the pale face of Artek, ruby red lips, full and proud above a slightly receding chin cutting his face like a knife. "I can't wait. I wonder how long it will take them to find us?"

"Well, it could be never, but with a little bit of help it shouldn't be too long. Let's not be in too much of a hurry though, there is still a lot to do, arrangements to be made, subjects to deal with." Malessa frowned at the thought of the pathetic excuses for citizens they had to make do with. The sooner her son and that girl were married and began producing children the better — then the new rule would begin and the world would be full of order. The future would be bright, regal, and everything would just be absolutely perfect. No loose ends, no Lethargy, just Whole people. Not Awoken people like her and her son; dutiful people; her people.

In their place, subservient and awed by the power of the immortals that ruled over them with an iron fist. All for their own good, of course.

Control.

Emptiness

It felt different to Letje somehow, different to when she had been out before looking for the others. It was truly empty now — the desolation was complete. It hung in the air like a thick fog, the absence of people palpable, cloying, as if the country was crying over its lost populace.

After the comfort of The Commorancy, the feeling of safety and protection by the most powerful men alive, being back out in the desolate countryside made her feel all the more vulnerable, worried too — worried for Arcene, for herself and Gamm, even for Leel, but more than anything she worried that she would fail, and the emptiness she felt all around her would only get worse as more and more people disappeared from her awareness.

They had been walking for days now, making their way to Artek's home, probably his old home now — the only real clue that they had to act on so far. It was a start though, a beginning to what Letje knew would be the most dangerous undertaking of her so far rather short life.

Knowing how powerful she herself now was, she still couldn't shake the feeling of vulnerability — a silent voice telling her that she was not up to such a task and Marcus had made a big mistake by sending them all on such a daunting endeavor. This was an undertaking more suited to those with much more life experience, those that were much more powerful than she believed herself to be so far. Yet Marcus and Fasolt had agreed, and she certainly wasn't going to refuse, knowing that Marcus had been right: above all else The Commorancy and its occupants, few as they were, must be protected.

Vying with her concerns was the pleasure of being away from the duties that had been hers, now resumed by Marcus. She had to admit that she was enjoying the company of Gamm, and although Arcene was as mad as a pond full of frogs it was nice to see her out in the open where she couldn't do quite as much damage — although she still tried. Yet again Letje marveled at the exuberance of her young friend, now doubled because she had Leel to goad her along, or vice-vera, it was impossible to tell really so she just left them to get on with it.

A Man Named Horse

The large group of horses bolted as soon as the young foal crashed to the ground, the arrow hitting its mark, the young horse's heart punctured and leaking out her life-blood. Ahebban came instantly to enhanced awareness via The Noise, bewildered by the fact that he hadn't picked up on the presence of humans until it was too late.

There will be more of the same unless you do as you are told, came a voice directed at Ahebban through The Noise.

Do I have any choice in the matter?

What do you think?

It didn't take long. In less than an hour the large herd of horses, many now directly related to Ahebban, were enslaved, and for the first time in countless generations they were at the mercy of man once more.

Ahebban had grown into a large stallion, densely muscled and at the head of his extended family. Since his consciousness had accidentally become trapped in a newborn foal he had tried but failed to save, he had grown to love his new body and the simple life that it allowed him to lead.

Now it was ruined, gone just like the innocent creature snuffed out by a man that cared little for life other than his own, his only concern how he could manipulate others for his own ridiculous dreams.

The man, Artek, had killed the young foal to make a simple point: he was to be obeyed. He knew Ahebban was Awoken, and once human, and had taken advantage of the fact to ensure that he, and those under his care, could be easily captured. Ahebban could have escaped, he was sure of it, simply run off, put up a virtual wall in The Noise so the strange red-haired man could not direct his actions, but what of the others? They would still be captured, just more violently, and more deaths would be the result, he was sure of it.

Ahebban did as he was told and calmed the jittery youngsters, still on wobbly legs and hiding behind their mothers. The adults acted as he directed, subtle manipulations given through The Noise allowing him to calm them without them being aware they were being gently coerced. The other males, mostly still immature as once adulthood came horses went to find their own families and mates, were a little more skittish and tried to resist, but soon the memory of the attack seemed to vanish from their memories. The man — Artek, warped reality somehow so they hardly even took notice of his presence.

They forgot, and Ahebban could feel the power of the man, becoming as if a ghost, there just on the periphery, enslaving the innocent to further his own goals.

Ahebban was left untouched though, merely told of what would happen if he disobeyed or failed to keep his herd in check.

What do you want with me? With us? asked Ahebban, once the herd were all tethered and many had already had bridles and saddles put on them.

You'll see. Just keep your herd in check and everything will work out fine. I won't mistreat any of you as long as you understand that I am your Master now.

There was silence, the man staring into Ahebban's large eyes, him knowing that he could kill the man in a heartbeat if it wasn't for the power he now held over him.

Well, I'm waiting.

Yes... Master.

~~~

The days, then the weeks and months, blurred into a never-ending repetition of daily routines, interrupted only by the difference in the people that were upon the backs of Ahebban's once proud and totally free herd. Now they were downtrodden, enslaved, made to carry all manner of men, women and children upon their backs — people held just as captive as they themselves were.

Ahebban abhorred it, often wondering if it would be better to simply revolt and have their lives ended — at least in The Void there would be no shame.

Every time they went out to collect more people Ahebban thought the same thing, and every single time he failed to commit to a course of action that would see such once innocent and wild creatures put to the slaughter because of his actions.

Maybe one day it would all be over? Maybe one day they would have their freedom again? He doubted it. But there would come a time when he would have his revenge, or he would die trying. For now he simply bided his time, did as he was ordered, and watched with shame-filled eyes as the fine creatures he loved fiercely became more and more subdued. The memories of their freedom lost as the drudgery of their days broke their spirits and they became nothing more than transport — no longer the proud and beautiful looking creatures they had once been.

It sickened Ahebban to the pit of his stomach and he often wondered if Marcus hadn't been wrong to try to fight The Eventuals when humanity was still so evil in so many ways.

Yet he knew that Artek was not how all people acted. After all, he had once been human himself. His accidental entrapment in the foal had been a blessing, allowing him to run fast and free through the countryside, revel in the glory of a frosty morning, the chance to commune with nature, fully understand the beauty of the world he had a second chance to experience in ways unknown to him when a man — even an Awoken man.

The more Ahebban and his herd went out on their regular missions, and the more time he had to endure the foul man on his back, the more Ahebban came to truly understand one thing: Artek was insane.

He was incredibly intelligent, Awoken and proficient in The Noise, able to do many things unheard of even in other people who became powerful after they Awoke, but at the heart of it all was an insane man with an insane mother and an even more insane plan and outlook on life.

The saddest part of all was that it seemed very likely he would succeed with his goal of ruling over the remains of humanity. A king with subjects that were either subdued or content enough to bow down to his rule, or be eliminated from the planet as they failed to obey.

Ahebban had seen it countless times, seen the way this would-be-king acted toward those that failed to treat him with the respect and subservience he somehow felt he was due. No, not just due, but deserved, had a right to: his destiny.

Completely insane, yet incredibly intelligent — a very dangerous combination indeed.

~~~

It must have been at least two years since Ahebban had first been captured when he truly realized just how much of a megalomaniac Artek truly was. It was hard to tell exactly, horses didn't really take any notice of such things, and as much as Ahebban clung to being human there was no denying that much of him was now truly equine — inescapable when you occupied another creature for so long.

He was a large stallion, the biggest and strongest of the herd, so Artek had chosen him to have the dubious honor of being his horse, a replacement for his previous mount — Ahebban didn't even want to think about what had become of those that had previously had the terrible task that was now his. Wherever they went, whenever they went out on another expedition to take more people away from the lives they had been leading, it would be Artek riding on a huge white stallion that was the first, and sometimes last, thing that the unfortunate people would see.

He knew how they looked, how impressive a sight it was, and he hated it every single time they rode up to a house, an encampment or a strange home that had warped the people living inside over countless generations until they hardly resembled people as they once were.

It was on one such expedition that he really understood the risk to humanity that Artek posed.

The trek had been a long one, much longer than normal, and already Ahebban was exhausted by the time they arrived at their destination. He could tell that the rest of his herd were feeling the same — you only had to look at them to see how obviously close to their limits they were. They had been fed well, they always were, but the toil of years of activity with not enough rest between expeditions built to a point where nothing would help apart from months of recuperation and a removal of the saddles, bridles and countless straps and added baggage that was their lot now, day in and day out.

Ahebban had lost count of how many people they had taken, only knowing that it was but a small fraction of the numbers as a whole. There were other horses, other herds, even other means of transport used if Artek or his mother, or one of the few trusted servants they had, went off to claim another person's freedom, leaving the country increasingly empty.

As the years slipped by and the number of murders and incarcerations as well as the strangeness of his new life increased, Ahebban became ever more aware of just how few people there were left with their freedom. They saw less people, he sensed less people via The Noise, and their trips became longer, more convoluted, and the people they took were much harder to find. Nearly everyone that could be taken was now locked up in Bridewell, that strange place where humans were silent for fear of death for disobeying their new ruler.

They had gone across country at a slow trot, Ahebban and Artek at the front, a servant behind on a large brown mare, followed by at least fifty more horses in single file behind them. Most from the original herd, some from others that had been integrated over the years since initial capture.

From their vantage point they looked down on a large stone building, a convent. All through the journey Artek blathered on about how he had found a strange sect via The Noise, able to pinpoint where they were, their minds almost alien they were so different to how humans usually shone in the intangible world that was The Noise.

Artek was incredibly proficient in that mysterious world and had a knack for uncovering even the smallest hint of human life. He followed all the clues, or directed his servants to do so, and slowly but surely the country emptied of living souls until there were hardly any left. The more people he took, the easier it was for him to find others — the less crowded the strange ethereal space, the easier it was for Artek to follow the sparks that signified a human mind.

They descended the grass covered hill, the wind whipping at Artek's always perfect hair, his green shirt and black overcoat flapping as he used his legs to move Ahebban into a gentle canter.

He was to go alone, as he usually did, the others hiding in a small copse until he signaled them to move forward.

At the front of the convent Ahebban could feel the minds inside, strange minds, some simple, almost half-minds: men that were almost like children or pets, was the only way he could describe the emanations they gave off. Others were stronger, female, and one was incredibly strong, shining brightly through the thick stone walls like a beacon that declared her power and her age.

She had opened the door and stepped out into the crisp air, the sun bright but weak as spring marched slowly into yet another summer. She was a tiny woman, a bizarre creature wearing a nun's habit that was faded yet immaculately clean, her large head looking out of proportion for such a tiny body. Behind her were a number of other nuns, all similar in appearance, and the men too, wearing simple work clothes, clearly second class citizens, much as Artek felt about everyone — servants, there to obey and act how he saw fit.

The diminutive nun was clearly powerful, her stature in no way reflecting her skills, but it was clear as soon as the conversation began that she knew little of the world away from her little bubble of religious servitude; she cared even less about it.

The meeting took on the usual form, reality blurring and the edges of consciousness fading until it was hard to think clearly about what was happening, what you were doing, what you were somehow being made to do. He'd seen it over and over again now and had a clear idea of what Artek did, although he was never absolutely certain — the captures were always somehow hazy, not quite sharp or in focus, reality warping and losing clarity.

But he was used to it enough now to see that the nuns were going to be no different to anybody else that had been taken. A conversation began that was friendly enough, with Artek subtly insinuating himself into their good graces by being gracious, polite, the perfect guest. Then he often left, once he had found out the exact number of people involved, whether he wished to take them or simply eliminate them, either to return with the rest of the herd and assistance from the trusted servants, or to return alone to kill before burying the bodies far away from their homes, leaving no trace of them or the acts carried out against them.

This time Artek didn't even bother with the charade for long. He was obviously intrigued by the strange group of people that the Mother Superior called The Sisters Of The Lethargy, but they clearly had no interest in Artek whatsoever — if anything they were more interested in Ahebban than the peculiar man that sat so regally on his back.

The conversation had not gone in the usual manner, the Mother Superior making it clear in no uncertain terms that she did not want to speak to Artek, did not intend to invite him in for a conversation, and in fact was considering exactly how she could eliminate him and lay claim to the fine creature he was sat upon. She was clearly resolute, and as she rolled up a sleeve revealing a hypnotic maze of bright blue tattoos that seemed to fray the edges of reality as she spoke strange words through needle sharp teeth, Artek took control of her violently, with little in the way of subtlety.

It was mere minutes later when Mother Superior was sat upon Ahebban's back, clutched tightly by Artek who sat her in front of him, and the large herd was weaving its way toward them to collect the rest of the inhabitants of the secluded convent.

All about them was a dream-haze of warped reality, a fog of forgetfulness, a distortion of what was real and what was but a mental manipulation. Artek had the power to make people forget, to change their realities to suit his needs. Ahebban could feel it seeping through The Noise, changing people's experiences so they were happy to do as directed, pleased to be a part of Artek's manipulated world. The Mother Superior was content to be sitting on his back, lost in a half-trance of forgetfulness, simply accepting her situation without a thought as to whether or not it was something she wanted.

The rest? They were easy to take — wrapped up in a thick layer of control that saw them lifted up and mounted three strong to each horse, tethered into place like little more than baggage.

The return journey was long, even more exhausting for the herd with the additional weight, and Ahebban felt sick to his stomach at the air of excitement and contentment that permeated the air — emanating from the mind of Artek that infected both horse and human in the immediate vicinity.

It was perverse, and there was going to be no end to such manipulations until this man that wanted to be king ruled over an almost empty kingdom, locking in an obscene dream-state those lucky enough to be allowed to live. The man seemed to see something really rather promising in the nuns, especially Mother Superior, and even Ahebban had to admit it was interesting to ponder just exactly how they had managed to survive for hundreds of years without a single one of the definitely inbred offspring ever succumbing to The Lethargy.

With his head hung low, the weight of countless lives hanging heavy on his conscience, Ahebban knew that there was no way in the world that Malessa would ever allow such strange creatures to be a part of the plans she had for her son and their future — whatever Artek wished. He may have been an exceptionally talented man, but he seemed to be lost in his own dream-haze when it came to his mother and the actions she directed, seemingly without Artek really understanding that it was not he who was in control of the cleansing of the country — it was her, the true ruler of what was fast becoming a desolate realm.

The Man who Would be King

Artek knew his mother wanted the power all for herself. She might try to act like everything she did was to help her son, to teach him the ways of their ancestors, groom him for his soon-to-be-total dominance over a subdued, waning populace, but he knew better.

She wanted it all; wanted to be in control of the dying days; keep the last of their people under her control until it all went away and all that was left was her, him, and hopefully the beginnings of a new, ultimately powerful line that would sow its seed across the country, then the continents, the planet — rebuild it all as she saw fit.

Well, she could think what she wanted, he had his own plans in mind, and the future he saw did not involve him being talked down to by her. She would be happy with the position he decided for her, or she could take her leave — permanently.

Ever since he had been a small child she had dominated his every waking moment, never giving him a moment's peace to play and just be a normal child.

"Normal? What do you think normal is? And why would you want to be that anyway? Oh no, you are destined for great things Artek, and I am here to see to it that they are achieved."

That had been her reply to him when he was just a small boy and said he wanted to just go out and do normal things like climb trees and play in the streams rather than learn about manners and the correct way to use the long line of complicated cutlery set out on the pristine white tablecloth every day for supper.

Yet on it went, through the years then the decades — her will imposed, Artek slowly molded into her vision of what a rightful leader should be, would be, was destined to be.

He was King, and he should act like one, was her opinion on the matter of his upbringing. She was right of course, he was actually one of the few people left alive that could trace their ancestry right back to the last Royal, although it was so far removed that it was as good as meaningless, or would have been if there had been anyone else left that could make a better claim to head the monarchy, the state, and therefore the country.

There had been hour after hour of tedious study, learning of his proud heritage, his royal blood, his right, her right more like, and although he had rebelled in minor ways over the years the truth of the matter was that Artek did feel like he had every right to subjugate the small number of people that would be deemed worthy of his rule.

The rest? Well, if they were found wanting then what use were they? Who wanted to rule over worthless creatures that would despoil what was sure to be a grand future dynasty that encompassed the globe? He would reign through the centuries, watching his kingdom grow and flourish, his name forever linked to the second wave of humanity — this time under strict supervision, never allowed to spiral out of control, take over the planet and spawn in their billions, unable to feed themselves and running wild.

No, that would not do at all. There had to be order, a system, a plan, and in that he wholeheartedly agreed with his mother — he just planned to do it on his own terms was all, and she had better not get in his way.

Artek smoothed down his immaculate green shirt, lifted his polished boots up onto the footstool and absentmindedly twisted his somewhat unruly mustache, a tiny sign of his rebellion against his mother's complete and utter obsession with order.

So far so good, things were going as planned. He was in no doubt that sooner or later he would be meeting with the new ruler of The Commorancy, and Arcene. It would be lovely to see her, his friend over the years that he had grown extremely fond of through their conversations. His wife, although she didn't know it yet.

They had studied her lineage, and although not ideal her French blood was of the highest possible pedigree. She would be the perfect bride for the perfect groom, the man that would be King soon enough.

He sat back and smiled, brushing invisible lint from his cuff, taking a sip of tea from his bone-china teacup before placing it delicately back on its saucer, the tiny rattle sucked up by the deep rich furnishings from bygone eras when people knew their place and showed respect for their betters. As they soon would again — well, those that he and Mother decided were fit to be ruled over. Already the numbers had reduced rather satisfactorily, and the culling would continue until all that was left was a small retainer to look after his estate as he went about growing his family that would rule for millennia, directing humanity's future in the best possible way.

Unhappy Nuns

Mother Superior, all three feet of her, was as cross as when she'd caught Sister Of The Lethargy Margarite chopping off the heads of the azaleas and kicking them into the bushes rather than picking them up and burning them. Oh how she had scolded her, didn't she know how easily the disease could spread? The leaves had to be burned.

It wasn't the confines of the cell that made her angry, after all it was better than the quarters she had lived in at the convent for her many years on the blessed planet, nor was it the food, which was perfectly acceptable, no, it was the fact that her males were treated just the same as she. Did these people not understand the difference between a Sister Of The Lethargy and a mere man? They were barbarians, and they even seemed to treat their own men in similar esteem. That was all too apparent as she became accustomed to their ways — how strange these unbelievers were.

Her razor-sharp filed teeth, bulbous head and diminutive stature, nearly got her sent to The Void as soon as they were discovered, but some rather fast talking and plain curiosity on the part of her captors had ensured that she, along with all her Sisters and even the lowly breed-men, were kept alive and taken from their home of every generation since The Lethargy and brought to this strange place where all the rules seemed to be as backward as the people.

Sitting on her cot, she scowled at the creases that formed black lines on her washed-out habit. "These people are barbaric. Not once in all my years have I had to walk around in such filthy attire." The words came out with a hiss, the air whistling between the sharpened teeth, a speech pattern repeated by every Sister, even the men, all inheritors of a warped progeria ever since the first male of the new line had been taken in by the venerable ancient Sisters, now long gone, beginning the new order back when The Lethargy began to take the unjust from the world. He'd been a relation of hers, blessed with the same stature and appearance as she herself had.

Still, she wasn't overly concerned, not really, for Mother Superior knew many things her captors did not. She was simply biding her time before revenge would be taken, then they would forever remember the time they dared to interfere with the daily practices that had kept her order flourishing in its own small way far longer than any of the once great religions had managed through the years since The Lethargy changed everything. Forever.

Her spiked smile spread through the gloom, calling out to the weak that were right now awakening to her call in The Noise.

It was time, and she had to admit that it was actually quite nice to be in a new environment after so long — adventure quite suited her, she thought, as she scowled once more at her dirty habit and anticipated how different the red-haired barbarians would feel once The Sacred Ink was put to work to teach them a lesson they would never forget.

Not long now my Sisters, said Mother Superior through the Noise, countless smiles revealing pointed teeth was the reply, as they looked forward eagerly to witnessing firsthand once again the price you paid for being anything but completely respectful to Mother Superior.

She adjusted her cornette, the traditional headpiece of her order, glad she couldn't see how dirty it would obviously be, the once crisp lines probably now faded.

She smiled. Soon she would make a new one, maybe out of the pale skin of that horrid man with his ridiculous red hair.

~~~

She may have been very demanding of her Sisters and the lowly men that served The Order, but Mother Superior was nothing if not patient. So she waited until the opportunity arose then put her plan into action. She would escape the place she somehow knew she wasn't supposed to like in the slightest, although as far as she could tell her opinion on her current situation waxed and waned on a regular basis.

It was most disconcerting, and she knew that she was being manipulated even if for the most part she didn't actually mind. Now she was lucid, somehow herself for a brief spell, and she understood that it was all down to Artek and whether or not he was exerting his control or had other things to occupy his mind. He would pay for his oversight, so would all those that dared to treat her and her Sisters like nothing more than common criminals. How dare they! The Sisters Of The Lethargy answered to nobody, nobody apart from her, and Him.

As the halls settled into shadow and the evening grew colder, Mother Superior felt the heat from her Ink warm her body beneath her habit. Even through the material she could see the swirls pulsing with their comforting blue light. She reached out with the energy drawn from The Noise and tendrils as delicate as the air itself weaved their way through solid matter until they found the mind of the sorry excuse for a human being that was their male guard.

Soon enough he came walking down the corridor, silent, none of his usual insults, no rattling of the bars and sneering at those he was tasked with guarding. He reached her cell and put one of the keys from the thick chain into the lock. There was a satisfying *thunk* as the heavy bolt receded; he pulled the door open before wandering back to his tiny monitoring station.

Later she would let the others out, but first it was best if she acted alone, dealt with Artek then his mother, then this simpleton that was certainly not going to be any bother and would make freeing her Sisters that little bit easier.

Mother Superior made her way down the now dimly lit corridor, scowling at the weak lights that stayed on from dusk to dawn, then signaled silently for the doors to be opened to the less imposing and stark corridor that led to the rest of the prison. She watched as the pathetic man in his cubicle pressed a button and the door swung open noisily. She felt the eyes of her Sisters on her, but silence remained — they knew she would be back for them, that for now they were safer where they were.

With Awoken powers that she had thought made her invincible against the manipulations Artek was very proficient in, she sought out the presence of the man and made her way down corridor after corridor, the ambiance improving the closer she got to the opulent quarters he and his mother, a disappointment to the whole of womankind, shared with each other.

Finally she was outside a door that was the only thing between her and revenge; she turned the handle without a moment's hesitation. She mentally went through checks on her own body and mind, ensuring that she was locked down tight, strong, resolute and closed to Artek's childish games.

A wall of comforting warmth greeted her through the open door, her bare feet sinking into deep scarlet carpet, the smell of a delightful meal just consumed permeating the air, the clink of a glass and the crackle of a welcoming fire the only noise as Artek turned to face her from a wingback chair, one leg crossed over the other, puffing to life something she hadn't seen for the longest of times: a cigar.

"Hello Mother Superior, come for another one of our chats have we?" Artek smiled deviously at her before she was lost to herself once more and took her place opposite him, just like she had done on numerous occasions, telling him of her secrets before returning obediently to her cell, never remembering the times the exact same foolish escape plan had played out before.

Just Like Your Mother

Artek would never give his mother the satisfaction of admitting to her that she was somewhat scary, but the truth was that she terrified him at times. She was not a woman that invited hugs and a feeling of comfort and safety, she was as stern as her clothes were crisp.

And powerful. Very powerful.

He knew that she could do things he could have only dreamed of before he took advantage of Marcus' hospitality and became truly Awoken, but Malessa's extra years meant she was always a few steps ahead of him.

Even now, having been alive for over a century and a half, he still felt like a little boy in her presence — her will and sheer dogged determination were humbling and often awe-inspiring. But most of all she was just plain scary. It wasn't her appearance — although always perfectly turned out she never intimidated by her looks alone — no, it was the pervasive air of being so much better than everyone else and deserving whatever it was she believed should be hers, that made her something altogether elevated.

Things were changing however. The years since Artek had become a truly Awoken man meant that slowly but inexorably, like the cutting away of the coastline, the fear and the insecurity slowly ebbed. He was a man that had always been confident in all things but one — he had been raised to know he was superior to others — and now the worry over what his mother would think of the way he acted was finally dissipating like a morning fog as the sun warmed the earth.

It felt like he had found freedom for the first time.

There was no sudden revelation, no snap of the fingers and a realization that he had been only half a man for a hundred and fifty years, no, it was a very gradual shifting of the mother/son dynamic that meant he found himself slowly taking charge of things and even talking back to her if he didn't agree with a particular course of action. Then one morning he awoke with a smile on his face and understood that he truly was his own man. He didn't have to answer to the slender, beautiful, imposing and terrible woman that he had spent more time with than would be seen as strictly healthy by any society — if there had been one left.

"Ha, who am I kidding, that woman is still as terrifying as ever," said Artek to nobody, as he dressed for the day. But at least he could stand up to her now, argue his case, do things the way he wanted and not cramp in terror, dreading that look, the one he would have once moved heaven and earth to avoid.

It was his growing powers, the things that had been stirring in him for what felt like an eternity. It never seemed to stop, something was always re-configuring, warping, metastasizing and changing forever the person he was, wanted to be, whether he wanted it to happen or not.

From birth he had been taught he was different to others: better. Something he believed with certainty was true. As he advanced through childhood and into his teenage years, then onward to become a man, there was no doubt that he had inherited genes soaked in Awoken abilities that often bubbled to the surface, and once fully Awoken his powers increased tenfold — a thousand. Even as a child he had been able to make people forget, make the few staff that meekly did as ordered by his mother forget that he had got his clothes dirty, stolen sweet treats from the generous kitchen, just so they wouldn't tell on him and he could avoid enduring his mothers displeasure.

As he aged so did the skill. He always somehow had the ability to make people forget anything he wanted, to warp what they saw as a reality that was just slightly skewed in his favor, but always just the small things, and always only events that involved him personally. Sometimes it would work, sometimes not, but since he Awoke it was incredible the difference it made. The second he left his Room in The Commorancy he knew that the conversation he had with Marcus would be forgotten in no time. Marcus would never recall that he had opened his door and left even though he wasn't supposed to.

Buttoning up his shirt he smiled at that — Marcus thought he had been so powerful but he still got beat by him. How satisfying, and where was he now anyway? Dead, his head chopped off by that fool of a man Varik. Now there was just a little girl in charge of The Commorancy, with Arcene as her child helper. Well, it wouldn't be long and all that would change too. His ascent was assured; he would have his bride to stand by his side and watch him rule.

Everything.

Arcene Gets 'Deathy'

Arcene felt invincible as only a fifteen year old with a very shiny, and very sharp sword could. The red tassel hanging from the hilt swayed to and fro as the priceless weapon from an era of Japanese culture now long gone sat comfortably slung across her back.

Marcus had taken Arcene to The Room For Weapons much to Letje and Fasolt's surprise. They both forgot that Marcus didn't really know her as well as they did, but this was a sure sign. Arcene... in a Room full of very dangerous and exotic weapons...? That would be top of the list of things not to do if you cared about all your limbs.

So it came as quite a surprise when they both re-appeared with all legs, arms, fingers, toes and psychical features intact. Marcus had said that Arcene had been very well behaved and hadn't pushed too many buttons or done too much damage to the fortified walls, and anyway, lasers should be fired now and then and the poison darts were probably past their best before date.

He looked paler than usual though, and Letje was sure that his cheeks were a little too red, as if he was trying to suppress fear and a little worry.

Arcene, on the other hand, was brimming over with excitement and was swishing and swashing her new sword around like it wasn't a deadly weapon liable to cut through flesh and bone as if it were paper. Arcene, Letje and Gamm had been given some wonderful choices for outfits for their trip, and Arcene had decided that if she was to have a sword then she needed suitably whooshy clothes to match. As Letje turned to look at her eager friend she couldn't help smiling at the young girl. She thought back to the first time they met — the scruffy thing she was, compared to what now walked beside her full of confidence, eyes darting here and there, searching for foes or clues, probably both. Or something entirely different; you never could tell with Arcene.

Her sword was in a simple scabbard tied over her shoulder, her tight vest showing off a lithe slim figure. Her silver pigtails bounced as she walked and her knee length kilt rustled delicately, although Letje was sure Arcene was exaggerating her gait just so it would swish.

Black knee length socks and sturdy walking boots completed the outfit, the overall look one of a serious warrior if it wasn't for the bright pink shoelaces and the little bunnies on the side of the socks. Arcene had used a few straps and pieces of leather that she found to turn her backpack into a suitable piece of luggage for Leel, so had managed to escape having to carry much apart from her sword. Leel seemed to actually enjoy the responsibility.

The dog had learned quickly to stand on Arcene's left as she was prone to whipping her sword out without warning if she thought she heard somebody in the woods or mistook a shadow for a would-be assassin. Letje and Gamm kept their distance — when Arcene got into her 'deathy' zone you had best stand well back. The weapon was more than capable of slicing you clean in half if you happened to be in the way of Arcene's less than perfect control of her new shiny object.

Letje watched Arcene's back as she walked behind her, the sun shining gloriously, giving Arcene a halo of orange, the tassel suddenly bouncing wildly as Arcene halted abruptly, Letje's reflexes warning her yet again to stop quickly before the sword was whipped out, eager to slice.

Here we go again, thought Letje, turning to Gamm, raising her eyebrows until they disappeared under her hair. Gamm just smiled back, as used to the sudden stops as Letje. But this time something was different, Leel took on a stance Letje hadn't seen before: hackles raised, nose pushed forward with nostrils dilating like a bellows, head craning on thick neck muscles as if the extra distance would make all the difference.

Arcene pulled the sword out, curving in a graceful arc, steel glinting menacingly. Arcene moved into a fighting stance and seemed ready to get 'deathy'. Letje went deep and fast into The Noise but there were no people present apart from them; there was no immediate threat that she could sense. So what was the problem? Had Arcene just reacted to Leel's sudden interest in scent, or had Leel reacted after Arcene? It was hard to tell, the two were already so close to each other each was like an extension of the other.

"Guess it was n—"

"Banzai!" shouted Arcene, dashing ahead at full speed, body leaning forward, sword held down with her right arm straight, blade pointing backward.

What's she doing? Doesn't she know that's the single stroke attack? She's been watching too much of that anime again. Letje's thoughts were interrupted when she finally caught sight of the creature rushing toward them — the sun had made it almost impossible to see, the red coat of the huge male deer almost as bright at the reflected light. As the sun dipped beneath the horizon Letje had a second to witness the battle.

The deer was massive, obviously old, and clearly quite mad. A huge beard of foam beneath eyes black and huge a sure sign it was no longer in its right mind. Then it's head was down and it was charging directly at Arcene, a splintered antler almost as long as Arcene's sword, and just as deadly, jutting forward on its now lowered head. Faster and faster they ran, Arcene screaming again as she moved at full speed, her kilt flapping wildly in the slipstream. The sword tilted slightly, the blade now facing the attacker although it was still trailing behind Arcene.

With a blink of an eye, they were past each other, Arcene down on one knee, head facing forward and bowed. The sword still trailed behind her. A second later the deer collapsed to the floor while it still ran, sliced in two down the middle at a steep angle. The front half slid to the ground even as the rear was still upright.

Gamm was by Arcene's side first. Letje knew she was fine; she practically glowed in The Noise. Gamm would know this too, he was just a gentleman.

"Are you alright?" asked Gamm.

"Nanahonme. Good eh?"

"Ugh, what?"

"It was kata number seven; I've been practicing."

"Well, you got 'deathy' finally, and thank you Arcene, you saved us."

Arcene got to her feet, flicking the sword to get the blood off. She stared at it moodily when it didn't result in a nice clean sword like it did in the movies she had watched. "Eh? Oh, you're welcome. Can we eat it?"

"Best not to, no," said Gamm. "It was obviously diseased, the meat is probably tainted."

"Shame," said Arcene, patting Leel, who showed no interest whatsoever in the creature that Arcene had slain.

Sack The Chef

Mother Superior ripped viscously at the tough meat — no match for her needle-sharp teeth. She spat out a sinewy piece of brown flesh through thin lips drawn back in distaste. The one thing Mother Superior couldn't stand was disrespect to the animals she and her Sisters consumed. It was why the chef at the convent was seen as such an important role: it was all about respect.

She tore again at the meat, swallowing yet almost choking on the flesh that went unhappily down her gullet. This was no way to treat a Mother Superior, no way to treat anyone, not even the feeble-minded men that seemed to be arriving daily even now after all this time.

Wait. All this time? Surely it had only been a few weeks hadn't it? If that.

Her oversized head shook, trying to clear a fog of memory-loss that somehow just seemed wrong. How long had she been in this cell? It was only a few weeks at most, but that didn't fit with how she felt in herself. Mother Superior decided to take stock of her body, her mind, her surroundings; everything. Something wasn't quite right here, it wasn't just that she was being held a prisoner. Her? A prisoner! No, there was something else.

Her mind felt sharp, at least in the present, but the past was kind of blurry. Not her whole life, just events after they had been taken, but she still remembered the kidnap. But everything since? All just somehow not quite fitting together right, like time was on a loop, or she was not even the one that had experienced the timeline she was on at all.

Her body felt alright she supposed, but she felt different, not running quite as efficiently. That would be down to one thing only: nutrition. The Sisters held food in the highest regard and although they lived simple lives they went to great pains to maximize how efficiently the body worked when the right nutrients were ingested. It was part of their belief system, their religion, their vows to tread gently and respect all that was given to them.

She could feel that her body was sluggish, that vitamins and minerals were missing, that her macronutrients were not as they should be. This could not be the result of just a few days or weeks of food not from her own gardens.

This was the result of months of inadequate nutrition, if not longer.

But how? Where had the time gone, and the memory of it passing? She was Awoken, she was Mother Superior, such things did not happen to the likes of her. She rubbed at the cuff of her habit in frustration, eyes unfocused then suddenly sharpening as what she had been doing caught her attention. The cuff. It was completely frayed; washed out; the wrong color. She stood and looked down at her one-piece garment, noting the hem was the same, and dirty.

Dirty! Such things hadn't happened in centuries. In fact the whole habit was totally gray from being treated badly when cleaned, and it was creased too. Such blasphemy! The caked-on dirt around the hem and around the cuffs was ground in and the result of months of improper cleaning, there was no escaping that fact.

She sat down and thought quietly and calmly about what to do.

Of course, that devilish man and his mother would pay for her incarceration and that of her Sisters and her men, but now she knew they had been interfering with her own private thoughts and memory? Well, the price would be terrible, but it would be paid.

~~~

"Look at her, the stupid creature. Doesn't she know she's been through this countless times already. It's like watching the same thing as last month."

Artek stared at his mother crossly. "That's the whole point Mother. If it wasn't for me then who knows what she would have got up to by now? You saw what she tried the other week, not that she remembers it now. It's so silly, she thinks she comes up with a great plan, not realizing I've already dealt with the exact same thing time and time again already."

"It's pointless," sulked Malessa.

"It is not! It's fascinating, seeing how people work, that they always come to the same decisions each and every time. That tells you a lot about the human mind, doesn't it? People don't come up with different ideas, they don't react differently if they think they are in a situation that is new to them when it isn't. That tells you so much. Plus I have learned a great deal about people and there is much to the world I have yet to learn."

Malessa stood and walked gracefully to the door. "And what, pray, does it tell one about people? Enlighten me, please do."

Artek sighed, sometimes she was infuriating. "Mother dear, it tells you that they are sheep, that they are not capable of breaking free of their own shallow lives. That maybe they are going to be good subjects.

Intelligent, but easy to control at the same time. Isn't that what we want?"

"No, it isn't. And besides, those nuns are really ugly, and I don't want our subjects to be ugly. Ugh, it's disgusting! Have you seen their heads and their horrid little teeth."

"Mother, you need to—"

The door slammed shut, she was gone.

"Good riddance," muttered Artek, turning back to the monitor, watching the familiar scenario play out as he knew it would.

Lost in Swirls

It was so nice to have a rest, to just sit and do nothing for a while, and that was exactly what Letje planned to do for the rest of the day. She had picked a bunch of wild flowers and was heading back to the house they were to stay in for the night. It was only early afternoon but they had all agreed that a rest would be just about perfect. They had traveled enough, half a day of relaxation would lift their spirits and rejuvenate their bodies.

Letje walked up the overgrown path toward the house, spying Gamm sat out the front of the ivy covered cottage, his huge frame spilling over the ancient but sturdy wooden chair. As she got close she noted that he had removed his shirt and with eyes closed and head tilted to the sun he was obviously soaking up as much warmth as he could.

He was such a large man, such big muscles, and so nice. She was glad he was with her and Arcene — what they would have done without him she wasn't sure. What color were his eyes again? She couldn't remember.

Damn, they were closed, he must be asleep. But what are those patterns? Arcene hadn't given her any hint that he was so covered in Ink, and details like that should be a part of the reports on Commorancy guests. They sure were intricate though, and the color, it was so intense. Were they raised? They almost looked alive.

They spoke to her. Whispered names she had never heard, told of strange rituals and the filing of teeth. Told of Sisters and the way The Lethargy had been held at bay. They called to her and pulled her forward whether she wanted to take another step or not.

Gamm snored on, his head tilted back, arms placed peacefully on the silver wood, thick forearms as gnarled as the tree from which the chair was made. Ink pulsed beneath the skin of his torso as Letje found herself drawn deeper and deeper into she knew not what. It wasn't The Noise, nor was it The Void, this was something else entirely, something active, a calling card, almost but not quite a mark of ownership, a signal and a death warrant if so commanded.

Letje found herself kneeling at the feet of Gamm, eyes locked on the impossibly simple yet complex patterns of shocking blue as pale as ice, as deep as the ocean, as they swirled and drew lines around the contours of his body like decorative armor that would protect him from enemies if only they locked eyes on the brands.

The Ink danced, pulsing brighter, like a perfect cloudless spring sky, then jumped off Gamm's body altogether. The patterns spun in the air in front of Letje, as if they were as lost in a dream-haze as she was. They rang out as loud as bells the size of houses, re-configuring into ever more dizzying and complex patterns that were infinite in number. They vibrated faster and faster, telling of things that were impossible to know, of faith and abstinence and gluttony and acceptance, of peace and sacrifice, oaths and Grace. They whispered as loud as a cannon, telling of the death of all things and the legacy of The Sisterhood.

Then they stopped, their lack of movement smashing the air like silent thunder, before they were once again nothing but bizarre markings on a slumbering man as a young woman knelt before him lost in a world that told of many things yet gave no answers.

A sleepy eye opened and Gamm asked, "What are you doing? Why are you kneeling there?" Gamm opened his other eye and fidgeted uncomfortably when there was no reply. "Letje? Are you alright? Letje?" Gamm leaned forward and shook Letje by the shoulder, the scar-tissue heavy skin feeling strange beneath his fingers: hard and lumpy like rocks in a bag.

"Fine, I'm fine. Your tattoos, I never knew you had so many. Strange."

"Oh, right, yeah. Long story. You okay Letje?"

"Great." Letje got to her feet, shaking away the strange visions, and went to put the flowers into a vase.

"Acorns Aren't Flip-Talkers...

...it's just so I will always know where you are. It was my fault that Varik found The Commorancy, did you know that?" said Letje.

"No. Ah, so it's not just me that did something naughty and got everyone into trouble?" said a rather smug looking Arcene.

"Well, no, I suppose not. But I didn't go about talking to strangers, telling them secret business."

"Oh, well, erm, yes, well. Hey," said Arcene, brightening, "why don't you tell me how this works again?"

Letje knew she was trying to change the subject, but it wouldn't hurt to go over it properly, so Arcene really understood the powers in the world she now lived in. *As if The Commorancy wasn't enough for that,* thought Letje, smiling to herself.

Letje paused for a moment, taking in all that had happened since she last stood on the broken road looking into the branches of the impossibly huge Oak.

The tree was once a perverted symbol of the beliefs of The Eventuals, forced to grow by a little bit of energy passed into it by Awoken members of Varik's now ex-church. Bird had been there then, as he was now, just on different sides. Now he sat in the thick gnarled branches of The Oak proudly, not hiding and spying. It had actually been him that had come up with the idea of the acorn, plucking it from the tree before landing on Letje's shoulder then dropping it into Arcene's hand. Leel had, of course, tried to nab it and run off, but Arcene managed to retrieve the somewhat slobber covered acorn and hold it tightly in a clenched fist.

As Gamm dragged the excitable dog away and they went off to explore the once impossibly busy stretch of road that allowed vehicles by the hundreds of thousands to move to, from, and through the heart of Birmingham, Letje and Arcene stared into the tree, then down at the acorn.

Letje placed her hands on the trunk of the massive tree and felt the connection. So many hands had touched the bark over the centuries, warping its growth, manipulating it into a symbol of nature's dominance over man, forcing it to grow and imparting a little bit of themselves into its very fabric, permeating every part of it from the smallest roots to the highest leaf, and into its fruit.

Letje gave something of herself to the tree, thanking it for the adventure that had been the result of her innocent taking of an acorn. The tree responded with thanks, a slow and silent swelling of gratitude for clean energy passed to it via The Noise. Energy that was not tainted by ulterior motives, that wouldn't force it to grow into something it should never have been. It was too late now — the tree was impossibly changed from its original course. It would always be huge, dominating the skyline for miles around, even greater than the crazy conglomeration of roads that still cross-crossed and spiraled around and up the trunk that slowly pushed the roads and bridges out of the way, standing as silent witness to the inexorable crumbling of the man-made maze it grew amongst.

There was a sadness to The Oak, a weariness and a heaviness that was impossible to eradicate. *Almost a melancholy,* thought Letje, as she gave just a little more of herself to try to undo a small amount of the harm that had been done to it by those who were themselves warped by the doctrine of The Eventuals.

It helped. Letje could feel the change within the whispers of the tree, the slow sentience waking just enough to feel the clean energy that was gifted to it. There was a gentle acceptance and an imparting of knowledge that took centuries, yet also took no time at all. Letje felt the years pass by in a blur of nothingness, the memories of the energies gifted to it every now and then, the manipulated growth patterns and then a return to the quiet.

It gave a part of itself in return to Letje, as close to thanks as such a different sentience could ever come.

Then it returned to its slumber, the clean life energy given to it ensuring it would live to see the comings and goings of humanity for many centuries more — if they happened to be around that long.

Letje had wiped a tear and taken hold of Arcene's hand, before throwing the acorn she held over the side down to the ground far below where it would one day grow into a fine but entirely natural specimen of the British Oak. Instead she pushed Arcene's other hand against the rough bark and passed through Arcene just enough energy from The Noise for Arcene to be able to cope with it and it flowed into the tree with a silent whisper of sleepy thanks. Letje plucked a new acorn from an accessible branch and gave it to Arcene, telling her that as there was now a little bit of energy that had passed from Arcene into the Oak it meant that the acorn would be a part of her now.

"I gave energy to The Oak, so it is a part of me and I am part of it. Make sure to keep the acorn safe and I will always be able to find you, as it is a part of the tree it will always be there through The Noise for me to find if I need to. That okay?"

"Oh yes, that's great," said Arcene, smiling at Letje, knuckles turning white from clutching her gift so tightly.

"Hey, don't crush it," said Letje smiling back. "Just look after it."

"I will. Promise." Arcene opened her hand and lifted the acorn to her mouth. "Hello, can you hear me?"

she said, then moved it to her ear. Arcene's eyes grew wide, then wider still, then impossibly huge. She stared at Letje, mouth agape, unbelieving.

"What? What's wrong?"

"You said it wasn't a flip-talker. I heard you, heard you talk then."

"No. Seriously?"

"Yeah. Do it again, do it again." Arcene lifted the acorn to her ear once more and smiled in wonder. She moved closer to Letje and hugged her tight. "I love you too Letje, even more than Leel."

"Um, well, thanks. We have known each other a little longer than a few days too." Letje couldn't help but smile; Arcene really did love that dog. But the acorn, she never thought that it could actually deliver her thoughts via The Noise direct to Arcene. It wouldn't be long before Arcene would Awaken — if this wasn't a sign of her responsiveness to The Noise then she didn't know what would be. Things must be changing within Arcene, and she would be a very powerful young woman if she really could use an acorn as a flip-talker.

Who would have thought of such a thing? Acorns as communication devices. Letje stared at the landscape around her, the splintered fingers of decaying monoliths in the distance, the remnants of a fast-paced society she never knew. She wondered what such people would make of the world she lived in; she supposed it would seem just as bizarre to them as their dead world did to her.

Letje knew she would never make it in such a society — all that dashing about, all those people, all that noise. How did they cope? How did they keep their sanity without time and space to breathe deeply of the fresh air and marvel at the deep dreams of the trees that filtered their polluted air and tried to maintain some kind of balanced eco-system?

Maybe they had been all crazy? Maybe that was how they survived.

Maybe that was why The Lethargy came and wiped the planet almost clean of people?

To give the chosen few a chance to finally take stock of what it was they were lucky enough to inherit, and maybe get it right with a second chance.

"Hey. Hey!"

"Huh? Oh, sorry, just thinking."

Arcene looked at Letje quizzically. "Not going off into a crazy dream again are you? You make me worry you know?"

"No, no I'm fine. I think that's mostly passed now; I feel back to my old self... Mostly." Letje smiled at Arcene. "Now, what were you saying?"

"Oh, just that Gamm is waving us over. Look."

~~~

"What is it?" asked Arcene, peering down at Gamm's find while he tried to keep hold of a very excited Leel.

"Leel! No, sit. Good girl."

Leel panted heavily, eyes never leaving the treasure, obedient yet obviously keen to grab it and run off playing with the shiny object.

"You aren't going to believe this, but it's a skull."

"Doesn't look like any normal skull to me, it's too shiny," said Arcene.

"That's because it's the Mitchell-Hedges skull. I read about it, it was priceless. It's made from quartz, carved from a single piece, it even once had an jawbone."

"Leel, no!" shouted Arcene, but it was too late. Leel grabbed the ancient skull in her huge mouth, ran to the edge, and then carefully dropped it over the side.

"Well, I guess we'll never know how that got here, or why Leel took such a dislike to it," said Gamm, clearly disappointed to never be able to get to the bottom of the mystery.

"Maybe some things are best left alone," said Arcene, patting Leel on the head, congratulating her friend for what the dog clearly believed had been a positive course of action.

"Maybe you're right," said Gamm. "Come on, it's time to go."

Strawberries and Cream

What Malessa wouldn't give for a day out watching tennis at Wimbledon, eating strawberries and cream, drinking bubbly and chatting with others of her class. Alas, those days were gone for good, taken away by The Lethargy just like everything else. Such a life was but a distant memory now, so far in the past it could be nothing more than the result of a fervent imagination, dreaming of a life where money actually meant something, where breeding showed and manners were all important.

Now there was nothing, but soon the past would rise from the ashes like a glorious phoenix — it was what she had spent the last three hundred years slowly but inexorably moving toward.

Forty two when The Lethargy took her friends, her gossipy, annoying, idiotic, stupid yet lovable friends, Malessa didn't succumb like they did, in fact the opposite. She Awoke spontaneously to a world full of wonder and endless possibilities, but with nobody to congratulate her. There was her husband of course, but he may as well have had The Lethargy for the previous twenty years of their marriage anyway — the man was an imbecile, they had only married because their parents felt it a good fit as both came from well-to-do upper class families and there was no doubt that the marriage had cemented a strong dynasty. So the future had looked bright, if somewhat lackluster. Then everyone died.

It was annoying in the extreme. Malessa had plans, and they were completely ruined. The Lethargy swept across the planet, but more importantly it swept away her plans. She was going to be somebody, her children would be the most powerful she could possibly make them. When she decided to have them, of course. But The Lethargy ruined it all, everything crumbled to dust, a kingdom full of future subjects was reduced to nothing, just like that. All gone.

Malessa's Awakening was a glorious affair — she felt it stirring inside of her, felt powers waiting to be unleashed, and she came to understand that maybe, just maybe, her hopes and dreams weren't completely ruined after all. The country may be different, may be chaotic and unstable, but she could deal with that, could maybe control the dwindling population a lot easier now there were so few left.

Malessa grew older, bided her time, waited for the right time to bear what she now decided would be a single child — a son, King-to-be that she could guide and encourage, to plant her family line that simply couldn't end. It must continue, flourish and become what it was always supposed to have been: Royal.

After more than a hundred years of making plans, building the right environment for her child-to-be, Malessa finally decided it was time to bear her child. She had mastered her body, learned the secrets of The Noise, and had halted her aging in her early forties. So much of her life had been spent dreaming of a glorious future, where she was given the respect she deserved, that time passed in a haze — she often found that years had gone by and she had done nothing but dream, tending to her bodily needs as if an automaton — there, but so far away at the same time she never even noticed the passing of the seasons.

From her carefully maintained storage facility Malessa inseminated herself with the frozen seed of her now long dead husband, a fool of a man but with impeccable ancestry and many characteristics she simply knew would be passed to her son, ensuring he had the correct heritage: a noble at birth.

Malessa kept a small retainer to care for the ever-expanding home she had begun to build years before: Whole that were rather simple, happy to serve as they had been thoroughly indoctrinated by the overbearing woman that at least kept them safe and gave them a role in life — something severely lacking for the majority of the remaining population. People were lost. Malessa gave a select few hope and security, stability in a world that had lost its way, old traditions mostly long dead; forgotten by all but her.

The small estate ran like clockwork; there was no other way as far as she was concerned, and as her child grew so did her plans. Why just Great Britain? Why not the whole world? There must be a way to travel yet still retain a semblance of comfort. Was there anyone left though? Would they be worthy subjects? All in good time, the boy had to grow to the appropriate age first. He had to prove himself, show she had made the right decision to put her trust in him.

He had to Awaken; the people had to be pulled from their degrading existence where chaos reigned and lives were wasted. They would work together, they would gather in the flock, deem who was worthy of rule, eliminate the rest. Take the trash out, leave only those that would see the country and the kingdom flourish in ways it never had when it was over-populated and nobody showed appropriate respect to their betters.

Well, all that would change. She would see to it that the old ways returned, where respect was shown to your superiors, where people worshiped their monarchy, paid their dues.

Above all else it would be nice and neat, controlled, everything in its place and a place for everything. She would put an end to the disorder and the rampant chaos. The country was out of control and it drove her mad. Didn't these people have any self respect? She knew the answer after living through so many centuries — the answer was no, they were imbeciles, thinking nothing of how they lived their lives. She would be sure to change all that.

And she did.

~~~

"What if I don't want to go?" said a rather petulant Artek, trying and failing to stare down his mother who stood, regally as always, in front of him, her mind obviously already made up.

"Why wouldn't you?"

"Maybe I don't want to be locked in a Room for who knows how many years, doing who knows what."

"After everything I have done for you, everything I am going to do for you, and you can't even do this one thing to help yourself? To help your mother?"

"Mother, it isn't like that. It is simply that I believe I will Awaken naturally at some point, and we have a lot of work to do here, plans to make."

"There will be plenty of time for that, don't you worry. And you may well Awaken naturally, you already have to a degree, but whatever else I think of Marcus there is no denying that he is an incredibly clever man and has everything at his disposal to ensure those that have it within them will Awaken. Now, no more arguing, I have much to tell you if you are to gain entry successfully and handle things in the right way once you leave. There are some things Marcus must never learn of, but we must also find a way to discover exactly how he does what he does, how that impossibly complex Commorancy of his works, and have the means to eliminate him if he ever does try to stand in our way."

"Yes Mother."

Artek listened to Malessa's plans for his Awakening and grew more and more excited as she explained just what he was to do and the kind of man he would be once he left his Room at The Commorancy.

It turned out that she had completely underestimated exactly what kind of man Artek would grow to become. He even surprised himself.

The Big Move

Artek returned to the cold bosom of his mother, the only family he had ever known, but more than enough as far as he was concerned.

He felt so different, so much more alive, that he thought he might actually simply burst open, The Noise spilling out of him, shining brighter than the sun, energy pouring out of him in wave after glorious wave. Who knew that it was like this to Awaken? So much more than he had anticipated. But he was special, wasn't he? So maybe it wasn't like this for everyone else. Maybe they only got a glimpse at the things he could see, the things he knew he could do. Within minutes of his Awakening inside his Room Artek knew that he really was special, just like his mother had told him he was.

He felt invincible and wasted no time exploring his newfound powers — he tried them out on Marcus himself. It was so easy, almost too easy; he really didn't see what the fuss had been about with the man. If he could manipulate Marcus himself then there really was nothing stopping him, was there?

Artek went home a changed man; a true man. He felt that he had been nothing but a child until his Awakening, but now he would truly be fit to rule. All that was left to do was to begin to clean up the country, and much as he disagreed with a lot that his mother said and did, she was certainly right that it needed a strong ruler. People needed order, a dynamic figure to look up to, to guide, and yes, to punish when the need arose.

He was up to the task, he had no doubt about it.

~~~

"Mother, we can't call it The Prison, that's so vulgar," said Artek, really wishing the move could just be over with. He wanted to get on with things, not take years just to relocate to where they could finally commence what his mother lovingly referred to as The Cleansing.

"Well I don't see why not. It was a prison, and it shall be again. Until we decide who we consider worthy of being subjects able to help rebuild the country properly."

Artek sighed. "Yes, yes," he said, waving her words away with a languid, somewhat limp wrist. "I know all about that, there is no need to repeat yourself. But do you really think it fitting for our new home to have such a poor name? It's rather depressing don't you think?"

"You do have a point," mused Malessa, still amazed at the difference in her son after just a few years away from her, until then, tight clutches.

"How about Bridewell, that's suitably elegant don't you think?"

"Hmm, that sounds just about perfect. Bridewell. Bridewell it is then."

"Good, I'm glad we could agree. It's appropriate I believe. It means both a prison and a reform school, which is much more in keeping with our goals, is it not? Mother?"

"Yes, yes, I heard you. I was distracted. Will you look at that fool over there. If I've told her once I've told her a thousand times to be careful with that urn. I shall have to tell her again I believe." Malessa went to scold the servant.

"I don't know why you insist on keeping the ashes of Father, it's been long enough now don't you think?"

"It's a reminder, that we all turn to ashes in the end my son. All that remains is our legacy, and our children. One day you will understand, when the time comes for you to have a child of your own."

"That won't be for some time yet, we have things to do. That can wait."

"Oh yes, I wasn't suggesting you find yourself a pretty little wife just yet. But there will come a day when you find her, and then you will understand, really understand just what it is to be a parent."

What's the Secret?

"How did you do it? What's the secret?" asked Fasolt, lost in the dancing eyes of Marcus.

"Haha, I wish I knew."

"You mean you can't remember? I thought you were the original, that you wiped the memories only from the other Marcus'?"

"Well, yes, I did do that, but it seems I must have done the same to me too." Marcus was looking uncomfortable, knowing what was coming.

"Then there could be more of you? It could never end. Off goes one Marcus into the deep, out pops another from behind a curtain claiming they are the original. How can you live like that?"

"I don't. As far as I am concerned I am the original. I don't know any different."

"Yes, but if you can't remember then—"

"Look Fasolt, it doesn't work that way. I am me, the original. If not, then I'm sure 'he' will be doing just fine. I am, after all."

"Are you?"

"No."

"Ah."

"Hmm."

Fasolt brightened. "Cup of tea?"

"Ooh, yes please."

"Sugar?"

"Let's go mad, how about two?"

"You got it."

Immortal Jellyfish

Marcus could feel himself losing his grip on his own reality, slipping deeper and deeper into the ponderous half-slumber of the blue whale his consciousness occupied.

It wouldn't be long and he would lose himself entirely. He could already feel the changes, the drifting away of the man that was Marcus, replaced with a greater sentience that was completely alien to human thought.

Marcus thought about his current situation, wondering in his slow way whether or not this was what he wanted for eternity. It took a week to debate with himself the best course of action, a deliberation that would have been only a few hours if his synapses still fired as they had when he was a man, not languidly swimming through the black icy depths lost in the half-life of dreams of the planet and the impossibility of breathing the air through lungs and walking on solid ground. Such things seemed bizarre even as he recalled they were memories of a life that was his only a few years previously.

So much was being lost; soon he would forget entirely. It was simply not possible for him to keep the personality he once had without his human form — the whale was just too alien an environment to inhabit and stay Marcus.

Yet what options did he have?

He could never return to a human form, how could he? The chances of ever even finding a human presence on the ocean was next to impossible, and forcing himself into another mind went against everything that Marcus believed in. He had entered and driven the bodies of thousands of Lethargic, but he couldn't contemplate occupying a mind-space where a conscious person resided — that way lay madness for both parties.

Thoughts roiled as slowly as the tide moving across the ocean, deep ponderous thoughts, and a discussion with his host ensued. The ancient creature understood that Marcus was slowly drifting into its consciousness; they would become one mind sooner or later. Both of them felt the inevitability of such a joining. It was one thing occupying small minds, but the vastly intelligent mind of the whale was different: there wasn't room for them both if they wished to remain as they had once been.

Then they swam through the answer and the two understood that there was a way out, a way for Marcus to become something more, something unique, to spread around the globe and live forever.

Is that what he wanted? Immortality? A cessation of what he was? Never to return, a diaspora of the planets oceans and seas, becoming not one thing, but billions? Marcus knew it was possible, his old guest had done something similar: becoming not a single mind but a hivemind of hundreds then thousands, lost in a world just as alien as the one Marcus was contemplating becoming a part of.

Months passed and he swam to the polyp breeding ground of the tiny immortal jellyfish. The minuscule creatures, no more than a centimeter across, had done something unique in the history of life on earth: they had achieved immortality. Marcus had read about it long ago and it had always fascinated him. Now here was the chance to live such a life, to become immortal and know what it was to grow old, then regress back to the beginning and repeat the process over and over until the oceans boiled and the planet exploded in a ball of flame.

Marcus became an immortal jellyfish colony and began a life so alien there was absolutely no chance of ever returning to being a man. He was lost forever, making his way around the globe on the currents that took him where they would.

~~~

"What you reading?" asked Arcene, peering over Letje's shoulder where she was curled up on the musty armchair, wrapped in a blanket, deep in concentration.

"Oh, you are going to love this, it's the kind of thing you enjoy." Letje smiled at Arcene, who was already getting excited and had forgotten Leel for a minute, who reminded her she needed a fuss by nudging her hand repeatedly until Arcene resumed her patting of the huge head.

"What is it? What is it? C'mon, tell me."

"It's a book about jellyfish, like the ones we saw on the shore. Remember?"

"Ugh, yeah. They were all goopy and weird looking. What's so special about them anyway?"

"Well, lots. But there is one kind in particular, according to this book anyway. The person that lived here must have really loved them, they have loads of books on jellyfish and all kinds of other creatures that live in the sea."

Arcene began to yawn. "Um, okay, doesn't sound that exciting."

"What? About immortal jellyfish? That's interesting, right?"

"S'pose. Tell me then," said Arcene impatiently.

"Okay, come and take a seat, and snuggle in, I'll tell you the story of the immortal jellyfish."

Arcene was soon tucked up in the blanket, her head resting on Letje's shoulder while Letje thought about how best to tell the story she had just read but make it interesting for Arcene. A fairytale, that was it.

"Turritopsis dohrnii, better known as the immortal jellyfish, was born one day, long, long ago, back before people were even alive. It found itself as a tiny little larvae in the ocean, swimming about happily, so teeny you could hardly see it. Then the little thing settled down on the bottom of the ocean and gradually it attached to the floor and became a colony, with countless little bumps that were known as polyps.

"Now, all these little polyps were tiny jellyfish in their own right, and pretty soon they detached and began to swim about the ocean just like when they were one larvae, but now they were fully formed jellyfish too. As they grew and aged they eventually became adults, and were quite happy. But they would die one day so they learned how to do a remarkable thing, something no other living creatures have ever been able to copy.

"They began to get younger, rather than older. They regressed until they were immature again. And as each of the jellyfish came from the same planula that gave rise to the polyps, they were identical: clones. Each of the countless jellyfish was exactly the same as the others. In time they grew so young that they were a planula once more, with countless polyps that gave rise to yet more jellyfish. And so it carried on all through the years. Some were lost, some were eaten or met with accidents, but as long as even one jellyfish managed to grow young again and give rise to more polyps then thousands of new clones of the original would swim about in the ocean, each exactly the same as all the others.

"They dreamed their dreams of impossible lives, content in the knowledge that they were never alone, that they had lived, and were living, and would live endless lives that were infinitely different yet experienced through the exact same set of cells. On and on it went, and on it will go, until there are no more oceans and there are no people or no sun or no clouds and everything rests where it should — in The Void. Hey, it's a bit like Marcus isn't it? Identical copies each the same but having different lives too? What do you think? Oh." Letje got up slowly and quietly, leaving Arcene to her slumber. Leel jumped up into the vacated space and managed to somehow wriggle under the blanket with Arcene before Letje was out of the door.

I wonder if she will dream of immortal jellyfish? thought Letje. *Now that would be a bizarre way to live and never die.*

~~~

Marcus was a million creatures. Living, growing old, regressing back to his birth then multiplying and repeating fractured lives over and over, never dying, countless copies of a man dreaming of being a jellyfish slowly forgetting their past and drifting in an endless ocean, finally never knowing of the life its ancestor had once had. Yet always something was there, telling of impossible lives when there was but one, and life was filled with worry, power and corruption of the human heart.

The dream never ended.

An immortality repeated in an endless loop that a man inhabited somewhere, somehow, but mostly the lives were just lived.

Over, and over, and over again.

What? Now?

"Are we all set then?" asked Gamm, slinging his pack over his shoulder.

"Ready," confirmed Arcene, saluting smartly.

"All good here," said Letje.

"Alright then, let's go. We have some nuns to track." Gamm smiled to himself, obviously amused by what was happening to him.

Letje couldn't blame him, it must be odd for him to be off on such a strange adventure with two young women. Well, one woman, one still a girl. Letje looked at Arcene, then turned and pointedly spoke to nobody in particular. "Does anybody need a pee before we go? The plumbing is still good here so why not make the most of it?"

"I'm good," said Gamm.

"Me too," said Arcene, heading out the door with Leel.

"Are you sure Arcene? It's going to be outdoor peeing from now on for some time, you sure you don't need to go?" Letje knew Arcene only too well — she could guarantee that within five minutes Arcene would be running off into the bushes moaning about getting a cold bum and probably picking a patch of stinging nettles to go in as well. She had got used to comfort at The Commorancy and had moaned a lot ever since they began their journey.

"Well, actually, um, hang on, won't be a minute. I'll catch you guys up." Leel bounded after her, the pair of them clomping up the stairs.

Letje and Gamm went out into the fresh morning air, breathing deeply of the perfume from the overgrown garden surrounding the cottage on all sides. Letje looked off into the distance, the fields waist-high with grasses and wild plants of all description.

"It's beautiful, isn't it?"

"Yes, lonely too. But hey, not at the moment." Gamm smiled shyly.

Letje smiled back at him. "I saw your tattoos; they spoke to me."

"What? What do you mean?"

"When you were asleep and you found me kneeling? They kind of transfixed me, came off your body. Well, in the dream or whatever it was, and they spoke to me. The nuns? They are with this Artek I'm sure of it. He has them, everyone."

Gamm didn't look convinced. "And the tattoos told you all that?"

"Well, not in so many words, but they kind of let me know things, without really telling me. It's hard to explain, but the knowledge is there. It's like how you sometimes just know things, does that make sense?" Gamm nodded. "Well, that's what it was like. They made me understand that they are in trouble, told where we need to go. We don't need to go to where Artek was when Marcus met him, his old home, we need to go somewhere else."

"And you know where this is?"

"Not exactly, no. But you do."

"Sorry Letje, I'm lost. I don't know where they are, where Artek is. If I did then I would tell you."

"No, that's not what I mean. I don't mean, you as in you, I mean you as in your body. Rather, your tattoos. Look, um, if I may?" Letje moved closer and put a hand on Gamm's bicep, rolling the short sleeve up over his muscle.

"Okay, but what are you doing? They're just tattoos. A bit odd, granted, but then that was a given with The Sisters. They were not what you would call normal people."

"Haha, who is?"

"Point taken. But what's the plan?"

"Bear with me, please. Now, look at your arm, the Ink, and turn in a circle. Slowly."

Gamm frowned but did as Letje asked, slowly turning in a circle. "Um, it would be easier if you let go of my arm now."

Letje blushed and muttered an apology. *Damn, what is wrong with me? I'm an Awoken woman able to sleep on mountains of bones and enter the minds of men at will, and I let myself blush like a little girl.*

"There, stop! See it?"

"What, what?" Arcene came rushing over, Leel bounding along at her side as always. "Whoa! Cool, look at your arm Gamm. It's... What is it doing?"

"It's telling us which way to go," said Letje.

"Well, I'll be... Who knew? Those nuns never said anything about this."

"I bet they didn't. Now, all we need to do is keep an eye on your tattoos, and as long as it vibrates like that then we know which direction to head in."

"Yeah, and we get to look at your muscles all the time too," said Arcene, smirking and giving Gamm's arm a big squeeze.

Gamm smiled broadly. "You two are quite a handful, you know that?"

"What, me too?" Letje feigned deep shock. Surely he meant just Arcene.

"Yes, both of you. Well, come on then, let my mighty arm lead the way."

"What about the rest?" asked Arcene. "Don't we need to look at the other Ink on his chest too?"

Letje had the feeling Arcene was growing up fast — she was going to be a full time job for any man that wished to spend his life with her, that was for certain.

"I think the arm is more than enough, don't you Arcene?"

"Okay, suppose so," said Arcene glumly, before she skipped off throwing a stick for Leel.

The Folly of Youth

"Do you still remember what it was like, back before The Lethargy?" Fasolt and Marcus were having a cup of tea; it had become a regular habit. Each morning they would meet in the kitchen and chat over a decadent two sugar cuppa.

Both men had taken a while to relax in each other's company as there was a lot of history between them, even if that history had played out with other Marcus' as intermediaries and most of Fasolt's activities had been done in a covert, yet terrible way. Their consequences were so extreme and far reaching there was no denying he was in large part responsible for the death of one Marcus by his son's hand, not to mention thousands of Lethargic by Marcus' own hand, of sorts.

It got confusing even for Marcus, and Fasolt still found the whole tri-person situation impossible to fathom — some things simply didn't make sense, even in the world they currently occupied.

"I do," said Marcus, "although it seems kind of surreal now, like it was all a dream."

"And this doesn't? I sometimes wonder which is the dream, this or back then."

"Haha, I know what you mean. But this is it, this is the result of what happened then. Well, The Lethargy anyway. Do you think about that, why it happened? How?"

Fasolt slurped his tea from his favorite mug. "I think about it. I've searched in The Noise for clues as to what it really is, how it happened, and nothing. I don't think we will ever know."

"No, me either."

The two men drank their tea happily, a contented silence for a few minutes while they were both lost in thought of the days before their world changed so dramatically.

"I think it was the way that the world was that sent me over the edge you know, not that I am making excuses. I was a bad man even before The Lethargy, not nice at all."

"That's in the past now, none of us are perfect Fasolt."

"Yes, but I was properly nasty. It's unforgivable. But what a world it was Marcus, I never could make any sense of it, and I was older than you, a man when you were still just a boy."

"And look at us now," said Marcus, smiling.

"Exactly," said a suddenly glum Fasolt.

"Hey, no point being melancholy. It is what it is."

"I've often tried to figure out people, and always failed. Our country was impossible to decipher. Not long before The Lethargy we were sending men to war to countries most people had never heard of until our government told us their governments were evil so we had to go help free the people. But then there were people even worse that took their place. And we were friends with some countries that were against the new rulers we helped rise to power, and on and on it went.

"I remember. It didn't make any sense to me either."

"And then things began to really turn sour here in the UK. You probably didn't know half of the people, but all of a sudden nearly all the celebrities I had known growing up were getting arrested for horrible crimes, many against kids. Terrible. Then there were the politicians, who seemed to get more plastic by the day. You could listen to a whole interview with one of them and at the end you realized they hadn't actually said a single thing, all just empty rhetoric and sound bites that left your head spinning and wondering why they had bothered to say anything at all."

Marcus drained his cup. "Another?" Fasolt nodded. Marcus poured the tea and added milk and sugar, speaking while he did so. "I was a bit young for bothering with politics, but I remember my mum moaning about similar things, before... Well, you know."

Fasolt nodded, hair spilling onto the table, threatening to topple the teapot. "I know. Everything felt a little out of whack when I look back on it now. Banks up to all sorts of crimes where nobody ever got punished, social media taking over the planet, celebrities and footballers becoming more important than kings, queens, or those out to try to help society. It all seemed totally normal, but looking back..."

"It was like The Lethargy was already there, right? Slowly warming up for its grand finale. But it wasn't, it was just how people were, how we were. We liked it. The convenience, the stuff, noise and the good roads and buses and trains and being able to get on a plane and travel the world. It had its good points."

"Yes, I know, but still. Oh, I don't know, I'm just rambling. It's just that looking back at it now there was definitely something that was simply—"

"Wrong. Something was wrong but you don't know what?"

"Exactly."

"I think most people thought the same thing, or at least maybe not thought it, but felt it. In the quiet times? When they weren't rushing about, working, spending money, escaping reality with entertainment. They knew; they felt it. Something was wrong."

Fasolt scratched at the taut skin over his belly, lost in thought. "But what? What was wrong?"

"The way we did things Fasolt. The way we built cities, the way we built roads in the wrong places, the way we relied on governments to take care of us. The overcrowding, the noise, the messing with nature, the way everything ended up tasting the same, or of nothing. The mass scale of crop production and the way we allowed syrup and sweet things to dominate our lives. The way people couldn't even look at a dead animal without feeling sick, but would happily buy it when it was chopped up into little pieces and packaged so it was unrecognizable. All that. More. So much was wrong. I remember seeing a thing on TV about these little balls coated in something or other that had chicken in them. You know, the sort of stuff you put in the freezer and all the kids and adults loved? Well, it turned out loads of them were filled with horse meat. And you think, gosh, how can that happen? Surely at the factory where they make them they have chicken meat, then they do whatever they do, coat them in the breadcrumbs or whatever it was, I can't remember now, and hey presto, you have your delicious snack.

"But it wasn't like that. This program? It showed you how they were really made, like so much other stuff. It was crazy. Meat would get shipped along with lots of other meats from a processing plant, sent to another country to be minced and mashed up then sent to another country to be coated and then go to yet another country to be finally packaged. Then it was back home to the UK where the chicken came from in the first place. Except now it was half horse, half chicken. They could have just killed the chickens and sold that. I couldn't understand all that traveling and contamination just for it all to end up back where it started.

"It was the same with everything: travel and compartmentalization got out of control. It was like everything had layers of bureaucracy to make the way the world worked impossible for anyone to actually understand."

"So The Lethargy came and took everything away."

"Yes, and no."

"What do you mean?"

Marcus took a second to compose his thoughts. "What I mean is that maybe we had it coming and we blew what should have been a new beginning. We learned nothing and messed it up. I messed it up, you, all of us that were left."

"Well, what was the answer then?"

"I have absolutely no idea Fasolt, none whatsoever. I thought The Commorancy was the answer, but if things carry on like they are then even that won't matter, will it?"

"No, I suppose not. Especially if there are no people left."

"So let's hope that Letje finds them, or I'm afraid that's pretty much it for us, for everyone. No more people."

"Gosh, aren't we a pair of grumpy old men?" said Fasolt, standing and suddenly brightening.

"Another cup?"
"Why not?

Almost There

Letje was exhausted. She'd forgotten just how tiring Arcene could be for one, and add to that a very large and exuberant dog, new company in the form of Gamm, and an actual mission that they had to complete and it made for utter exhaustion of the mind and body. At least, it did for Letje, Gamm too. Arcene and Leel on the other hand showed no signs of slowing down or taking a more sedate approach to their search.

They were like a pair of kids off on a little adventure, rather than involved in something that could mean the difference between the end of the population or a continuation of life for those still hopefully lucky enough to be alive in the United Kingdom.

Day after day it went on, trudging through the countryside, following roads long ago reclaimed by the forests that covered the country, Letje getting more and more tired, Gamm getting short-tempered at times even though he was an incredibly sweet man, and Arcene and Leel skipping about like carefree kids, running this way and that. The pair never tiring until the end of the day, when they would greedily eat whatever was put in front of them, usually a kill made in the day by Gamm, asking for seconds, Arcene chatting away about the adventures they'd had before they finally fell asleep huddled together — inseparable even when still.

Letje didn't know where Arcene got the energy from — she'd always been wild, and definitely hyperactive, but the presence of Leel seemed to have driven her to new heights of craziness.

It's because she's got a new friend, one that follows her everywhere she goes. She loves the dog so much; it's what she's always wanted.

It was true, Arcene loved dogs and was simply beside herself with joy that she had a companion that she could dote on so much. Leel was a very devoted creature, Letje had to admit, and there was no doubt that they were perfectly suited to each other. Both were keen to always be on the move, to play and to explore like the world was brand new — everything needing to be inspected, tasted, sniffed. They were unstoppable from morning to night — when they thankfully curled up early and left Letje and Gamm to talk quietly by the side of the fire until exhaustion took them too.

But they got ever closer, Gamm's tattoos guiding the way, although they were far from the perfect guidance system. Often they had to change direction, realizing that the light had been fading somewhat and they had strayed from their path, maybe by days if not longer.

Day after day it went on, then week after week, until Arcene and Leel eventually began to become more subdued, the excitement of the trip replaced by the realization that this was serious and it wasn't just an excuse for them to have fun and explore the countryside. Arcene had grown up wild, mostly by herself, so had a true affinity for the outdoors — it was where she belonged, what had been the only constant through her formative years. It was clear that she felt at home in the open spaces and the woods, away from the wonders of The Commorancy, in a place where she understood how things worked. Where thankfully there was a total lack of things with knobs and pulleys, or strange contraptions that she always somehow managed to bring to life in the most dangerous of ways.

As they settled into a routine of walking, eating, sleeping and hunting, Letje came to understand just how much the natural world meant to her too. Living in The Commorancy all those years had occupied her completely, but being back out where life was simpler and everything was how it should be, she came to understand just how much it was a part of her. It was like everything was settling into some kind of equilibrium, and although she certainly had a lot of responsibility resting on her still young shoulders it wasn't the same as actually being in charge. There were no guests to greet, no Rooms, no clothes to think about, no maintenance duties — everything that went along with being the caretaker of The Commorancy. There was just her and her companions, the ground beneath her feet, the sky above and the need to eat, drink and sleep.

Simple. Things were less complicated; actually made sense. It was freedom.

It wouldn't last; it couldn't.

They had crucial work to do, and as the feeling of getting closer permeated the air, so they all settled into a routine that became stricter the closer they got. They were up early every morning, ate a light breakfast, even Arcene, then they packed away their gear, hid the signs of their camp, then walked until the evening, stopping only briefly for lunch, sometimes eating it on the move, depending on energy levels and how easy or hard going the terrain was.

On it went, day after day, muscles aching, feet sore, bellies rumbling, progress made, none of them knowing what it was they were going to face when they finally made it to the end of their journey, where the real work would begin, whatever that may be.

Letje thought more and more about it the closer they got, unsure what to do, how to act, what was waiting for them.

Would it all have been a waste of time? Were they going to find nothing but a dead nun and no sign of Artek or the people he had been stealing for years now?

It was impossible to know, so all they could do was make good speed and find out what waited for them at the end of it all.

Immurement

Marcus was in The Coffin Room, locked inside a metal box with no means of exit.

He was buried alive.

It was nice and peaceful.

Marcus felt relaxed, calm. His thoughts were clear. He'd had to escape, just for a little while. Even though he had spent most of his life experiencing more than any other person on the planet, he was getting that strange feeling again of never actually having really, truly been there — the one that had actually been running The Commorancy in duplicate for so many years. Once more the firsthand, visceral reality had struck home; he needed time alone.

It wasn't as if he was in a crowd of company, it was only him and Fasolt, and they often went days between seeing each other apart from the morning cup of tea, but Marcus guessed it was just the knowing that he could bump into Fasolt at any moment that was making him if not uneasy, then just a tiny bit on edge.

Now he was safely buried, with the timer set for two days and absolutely no chance of him getting out early. He had the clarity of mind to understand why he had made such an escape: he'd been alone for hundreds of years. Locked in his mini-Commorancy, unable to get out, waiting for his release, he'd not actually really, truly spoken to another human being for his whole stay. At the time he believed himself busy in the way only a man experiencing three lives could be, but that just wasn't really the case, not when you got right down to it.

Marcus still couldn't explain it, as the truth was he'd done everything the other Marcus' had, and it genuinely was as if he'd been the one doing whatever it was they happened to be doing at the time, but still...

Knowing such pointless speculation was getting him nowhere, Marcus put such thoughts aside, understanding it was an impossible conundrum that would never have a satisfactory answer, just glad that at least he'd led such a life, certain on a cellular level that it was but a tiny section of his existence as a whole, whatever that might already be for one of the Marcus' and whatever it might be for him at some point in the future. He knew adventure awaited him, and the fact that he didn't know exactly what it would be was a blessing he would be forever grateful for.

So much of the future he was a part of was there for Marcus to live as if for a second time — having already seen countless timelines spread out in front of him like pieces of string all diverging slightly, knowing that as each event happened a certain future he could see, usually clearly, would play out. That got boring. Really boring. What was the point?

But now? Now there were countless possibilities. This Artek, he'd changed it all — the fact that Marcus had been somehow made to forget the man meant that any futures Marcus had already seen and thought the most likely were simply nothing but a cosmic slight of hand, as the future would contain if not Artek himself, then certainly events influenced by his actions.

Marcus let thoughts wash over him, feeling them pass, watching as if they were nothing to do with him, a mere collection of images as if witnessed on a flickering monitor, just passing by, no need to grab hold of them and look at them too deeply. Soon they faded and Marcus felt the closeness of The Void, the emptiness that was at the heart of everything, what made everything function yet was a nothingness, at the same time containing every possible life and death that there had ever been and ever would be.

He let his mind drift on the cusp of the non-place, neither experiencing or not experiencing any of it, just being and not being there, out of time and place, a non-man.

Such an experience, or lack of, could go on indefinitely, a timelessness that had no start or finish. Only his body would dictate the length of his stay if he wished to remain.

Slowly, after just a day, Marcus allowed his mind to think once more, to experience, and to feel the metal box he found himself buried in, his future controlled by an electronic timer he really hoped still functioned.

He smiled in the dark, already feeling renewed and invigorated, with a new sense of being grounded, of being able to cope with the present, the past and whatever it was that the future would hold.

As his entombed deadline approached he realized one important thing, just before he heard a gentle *click*, and the door sprung open: he was rather looking forward to this new world he'd finally been allowed to experience.

While he climbed out of the coffin Marcus wondered how Letje was getting on. He wondered if she'd been captured yet, how she would then get the better of Artek, a man that was going to be extremely slippery indeed to deal with, as you'd simply forget that he'd even been there.

Marcus' eyes danced through countless shades of blue; he smiled as he padded across the bare floor.

I wonder if Fasolt fancies a cup of tea.

Already Taken

"No Mother, she won't do at all," said Artek.

"You can't deny she is an exceptionally pretty woman though, can you?" Malessa admired Umeko's flawless skin, her beauty shining out even in the gloom.

"I didn't say she wasn't pretty, but she's old. You know who I intend to marry and I won't hear another word said about it. This one," Artek pointed dismissively at Umeko, "will do well serving in my household, maid to my bride, but she will not be my betrothed."

"But—"

"Not another word." Artek stormed out of the cell, Malessa following behind, turning in the corridor to stare at the radiant woman one last time.

"So beautiful," she whispered, before she signaled up to the guard booth and the cell doors slid shut with a clang, leaving Umeko in peace once more. She could have locked the door with a key but such menial tasks were certainly beneath her station.

~~~

The rather dismissive encounter had taken place months ago, but every time Umeko saw the man or his mother striding haughtily down the corridor, never bothering to turn in her direction, she remembered the meeting with a shudder. It seemed that she had been forgotten about now, or was simply not worth talking to until the man had his wife and Umeko would come in useful to them.

Umeko had the distinct feeling she would be very fortunate to have any kind of future at all if it was down to the spoiled brat of what she could only think of as a boy in a man's body.

In the meantime she had little to occupy her time and even less idea how much time had actually passed since she had been taken from her family and friends then moved to the prison, for that was what it was: a vast, depressing, echoing prison full of silence, fear and loss. So much loss.

When Umeko first arrived the level she occupied had been rather rowdy, but that had soon changed as the cells began to fill up. One morning they were all filed out and told to stand in front of their cells before very clear instructions were given to them all as to what was expected of them and what was permissible.

Nothing, it seemed.

They were to be quiet, not talk unless directly instructed to, and were to remain in their cells at all times. No exceptions unless they were called upon by those in charge, and those in charge appeared to be the very odd mother and son that looked so similar yet seemed to bicker constantly with each other. It therefore seemed strange that they were at the same time inseparable.

Umeko felt like she would lose her mind.

Some of the new prisoners, for there were many just on her level and who knew how many in the sprawling edifice she had seen as they arrived, had begun to shout and scream after they were put back into their cells, until the mother had shouted in anger from her safe position out in the main corridor that the punishment for disobeying orders was death — there was no room for dissent in the new world they now belonged to. Loyal subjects were all that would be tolerated.

Sneers and catcalls were her reply, so she calmly and methodically walked up to each and every cell and shot the few that dared to answer back to her.

Silence.

It didn't last.

People broke. They cried, shouted, screamed and banged about in their cells. Each of them was eliminated. First it was the woman, then the son, then a new gruff person that never spoke, just went to any cell whose occupant was making a noise and dealt with them. It wasn't always as nice as a bullet to the head either, that much was obvious by the prolonged screaming and begging for mercy that often went on for hours before they were finally dispatched.

It was a nightmare, one that seemed like it would never end.

Soon enough most of the cells were empty; no noises echoed down from other levels or from distant wings of the vast prison.

The Cleansing was mostly over it seemed, and Umeko couldn't bear to think about what the killing had done to the tattered remains of humanity clinging to life in the British Isles.

From the shouts, screams and various regional accents before they were silenced, it was obvious that people had been taken from all over the country. All were Whole, some were Awoken; now most were gone. It wasn't even only those that disobeyed that were sent to The Void: the reality was that you were liable to forfeit your life if you were deemed unattractive, unfit for purpose — whatever that was — or they simply didn't like the look of you or believed you may be trouble in the future.

Umeko hated herself for praying that she would be left to live while others died, but she had her family — prayed she still did. Nobody had told her what their fate was, or that of her friend Kirstie and her young son.

She couldn't ask or she would be dead, then certainly never able to find out.

Umeko struggled with her memories. She knew that things were not right, not linear as they should be.

Everything was jumbled, so many pieces missing, like she had been replaying the same events over and over again, but never sure if she was just getting a feeling they had or if they truly had been. There were whispers of memories where she had escaped, or at least got as far as outside her cell, but had been captured easily and put back inside, the memory forgotten, just hints as if it were a dream. That man, that red haired man, it was to do with him she was sure of it.

Her Awoken powers and knowledge seemed of little help in her current situation, as if there was a jam on what she should be able to accomplish. Looking inside she could feel the control she still had over her body, it was absolute, but The Noise, a sense of The Void? Almost inaccessible, and she certainly got no signals through The Noise of other people, even her family and friend. It was as if they were being held back from her, their strong presences in her past wiped out, or hidden.

Umeko suspected the latter, or maybe she was just trying to convince herself of that? The alternative simply wasn't an option: could they be dead?

No. They couldn't be, that would be too much, not after everything she had gone through, the life they had lived.

Here it comes again, thought Umeko, lying back in her bunk, knowing from past experience it was futile to try to fight the memories of a better time and the fragmented memory she had of when it all came crashing down around her and her beautiful, perfect life turned into a nightmare in the space of one afternoon on a day that had begun just like so many others: perfectly.

~~~

Umeko and Ryce slowly grew to know each other, even though they had married the day after meeting. Some things just felt right, and she knew as well as he did that they were meant for each other.

It didn't even feel strange in the slightest: sharing her bed with a man she really knew hardly anything about. Over the months they became more intimate than Umeko had ever been with another person.

The baby grew inside her. Her Awoken state meant that finally she could have the one thing in the world she wanted more than anything else: a baby. Kirstie lived with them on the small farm that Ryce had lived on alone, her child learning to walk there and speak his first words. Soon enough there were two children and Umeko couldn't imagine anything that could make her happier.

It was hard work, there was no denying that, but finally she wasn't alone and every morning as she rose to care for her child she smiled at the good fortune that had befallen her. Every day she was careful to maintain her beauty regime, showering, using her precious creams from a culture long gone, and applying light makeup to bring out the beauty of her perfect plum complexion. Her cheeks were highlighted with a brushing of red, her lips likewise. She didn't need it, her perfect features were startling and always had been since she was as young as her own child.

There were also the exercises, those she had learned in The Commorancy, then perfected. She didn't look a day older than when she had first become truly Awoken and never would as long as she spent a few minutes daily practicing the techniques that allowed complete regulation over her body.

Life was perfect.

Hard, but perfect. She loved it. Having spent years roaming the country before finally getting accepted to The Commorancy, Umeko now reveled in the busy life of surviving in the countryside. There was the baby to care for, the household to maintain, endless chores from collecting eggs to tending the gardens and orchards — it brought a sense of peace and fulfillment she had been searching for her entire life.

Then it shattered in an instant and life became a waking nightmare of repetitive captivity.

Ryce had been out in the fields that curved upward into the hills away from the flat land around the farmhouse and buildings. There was a lot to be done now that winter had slowly made way for what promised to be a warm spring and summer. The ground needed preparing for the crops to be sown, so

Ryce was working long hours and taking advantage of the increased daylight.

As she scattered feed for the hens, taking their eggs in fair exchange, she could see him off in the distance. *Probably stressing over the pH of the soil again*, thought Umeko, smiling. He really did obsess about it. But he had a magic touch — the animals they kept gave a rich manure that meant the fields produced crops in abundance and he had said that now that there was a true family living at the farm the soil seemed to produce better crops year after year.

Umeko raised a hand to shield her eyes from the sun, making out a figure coming over the brow of the hill. At first it looked like just one of the wild horses they saw on occasion — Umeko often mused about whether it truly was just a horse or there was a human consciousness trapped inside, just like Ahebban that she had met in what felt like another lifetime now. Which reminded her, she must get in touch with Letje soon, it had been too long.

As the creature approached, Umeko realized it wasn't just a wild horse but there was a person sat on it, expertly guiding it down the meandering path that wound its way to the farm. She hoped Ryce saw the person and hurried back home, he was alone out there and who knew who this person was. Although encounters with people were extremely rare it didn't mean that everybody was friendly, yet Ryce never took a weapon with him when he worked in the fields, even though Umeko had reminded him on countless occasions until she gave it up as a lost cause in the end.

She saw the horse stop, the figure dismount. A man by the looks of it, although it was hard to tell. Umeko went to warn Kirstie — there was no knowing who this stranger was, so it was better to be safe than sorry. Weapons too, the women knew how to use them, probably better than Ryce. He was just a big softy really, even if he was pretty tough looking with his wild hair and always slightly scruffy beard.

~~~

"What man?" asked Umeko, confused.

Ryce stared at her quizzically. "Are you joking? The man that just left." He waited for Umeko to answer... "Come on, he left like a few minutes ago, you're telling me you don't remember?"

"I don't like this game Ryce, stop it. What are you talking about?"

"Look, I'm not playing. How can you not remember? Lanky guy, green shirt, spotless clothes, bright red weird hair. He just left Umeko. We had a drink and chatted for an hour and then he left. You can probably still see him," said Ryce, getting up and moving over to the window. There was no sign of him.

Umeko rocked Ella gently when she began to stir, it wouldn't be long and she would be awake and wanting to play.

"Hey guys, what's up?"

Ryce turned as Kirstie and Dale came into the room. "You talk like you weren't just here a minute ago," he said accusingly.

"What do you mean, I've been off playing with Dale. I haven't seen you since this morning," said a confused Kirstie.

"Are you two playing some kind of a game? Next you will be telling me you didn't just meet that man who just left."

Kirstie stared at Ryce, then turned to Umeko. "What's he talking about? What man?"

Umeko shrugged her shoulders. "I don't know, Ryce seems to think we just met some man with red hair."

"What?" said Ryce. "What man? I never said anything about a man."

Umeko and Kirstie exchanged worried looks. "Ryce, are you feeling okay? You just this second said we had all met... Um, where was I?"

"No idea," said Kirstie. "Anyone hungry?"

"Eh? What? Oh, yes, I am. I'm starving," said Ryce.

"Me too," agreed Umeko.

~~~

It wasn't until months later that the conversation came back to Umeko. Then she remembered that they had all sat around with the man, talking and drinking. He seemed nice, in an odd sort of way. Then he had left.

Then he came back and Umeko couldn't remember any of it. All she remembered was arriving at the gates of a huge sprawling prison in the back of a canvas covered vehicle, wandering in a daze through corridors before finally being ushered into a cell. She never even knew she had a baby or a husband until days later, she had somehow managed to forget all about them.

She's Old Enough

Artek and his mother watched the monitor closely, tracking the progress of Letje, Gamm and Arcene. His bride to be was almost here; he couldn't believe it.

"I'm so excited, she's almost home. Almost mine."

"She is a pretty little thing isn't she? If a little coarse. Not exactly ladylike."

"Mother, she is only fifteen and look at the life she has led. The poor thing was all alone out there in the wilds for a long time, then after that she has been locked up in The Commorancy. What do you expect?"

"I would prefer that she had some manners," said Malessa, turning her nose up as she watched Arcene skipping about, playing with Leel.

"Well, soon enough you will be able to teach her how to act appropriately, won't you? I'm sure you will enjoy it immensely."

"I wouldn't go that far, but yes, I will teach her how to be a proper lady, how to act in the right manner.

And that dog will certainly have to go, we can't have her stinking like an animal if she is to be Queen, now can we?"

"Hmm, we shall see. All in good time. For now I just want my Arcene to be happy. If that means the dog has to stay for a while then so be it. I can't believe she is finally going to be mine though. I feel like I've been waiting my whole life for her even though it seems like only yesterday that I first spoke to her. It's been what, four years or so now?"

"About that I suppose. I must say that you really did take your time finding yourself a wife, I was beginning to get worried."

"I told you, nobody suitable ever showed themselves to me, then I found Arcene and she was just about perfect. I simply had to have her the moment I first set eyes on her. Even though she was only a child then I knew, I just knew that she was to be my wife." Artek paused before repeating, "She is just about perfect."

"We'll see."

Artek stared at the screen, eyes shining, grinning like a child that had been given the best toy in the whole world. He still looked exactly the same as the day he left The Commorancy, a young man in his prime, not a man of over a century and a half in age. Artek had not only chosen to keep his body the same age as when he Awoke, but it often seemed that his mind had halted then too — in many ways he still acted like a spoiled child, not a man with more life experience than previous generations could have dreamed of.

Malessa stared at her son, wondering not for the first time if he had ever really become a man at all. Or would he forever remain a child no matter how many years he ruled over a kingdom she had arranged as the ultimate gift for the boy that had almost everything.

~~~

"I want her."

"There are a number of more suitable women that I have in mind, and they are more mature."

"No, I want Arcene. She may be young at the moment but in a few years she will be of age. I want her to be my Queen, no other."

Malessa knew better than to argue with her son over such an important matter — once he made his mind up then there would be no changing it. Maybe he was right, maybe she would be suitable to be a daughter-in-law and rule by Artek's side.

Artek had seen her when Arcene was but a scruffy, unkempt little child, far removed from what she was today, but bizarrely Artek didn't seem to mind. He'd kept track of her through countless adventures, never interfering, knowing that however much he wanted the strange child to be his wife once she was of age, it wouldn't do to have somebody that couldn't take care of themselves — this was something he agreed with his mother on. So Arcene had been watched, infrequently at first, more and more regularly as she grew older, and once inside The Commorancy Artek had begun to find a way to infiltrate the girl's life so he could begin to get to know her.

Purely by chance he happened to be there when Arcene was playing with the equipment that allowed a conversation to be possible — it could have been any number of other ways he finally made contact, after all he was monitoring bandwidths, trying to find ways to hack into The Commorancy through their network, but without a good place to start he'd found it impossible. He accessed Commorancy web pages and the announcement boards that were occasionally updated, all in a vain attempt to begin a conversation, but the timings were never right and it came to nothing. Then, one day when he was simply running through his usual checklist he'd heard her voice, loud and clear, a confident "Testing. Testing. One, two, three," and with a "Hello, is anybody there? Who's this?" Artek knew he had his way into her life.

What he learned about Arcene and about The Commorancy was invaluable. He couldn't believe the passwords used, which were incredibly simple to discover once he knew just a little bit about the people occupying it, managing to get access through offering to help Arcene with some of the more difficult aspects of her work keeping records up-to-date for Letje. He mined, copied and read as much as he possibly could, until finally he was discovered by Letje — it didn't matter, he'd already taken what he wanted, and above all else that was to get to know Arcene.

He wanted to be sure that once she did arrive, and he knew she would, along with Letje, once he was discovered, that everything was just right for his future bride. He wanted to know what her likes and dislikes were, what she enjoyed doing, and what she liked to eat, something he found was rather easy a need to satisfy — Arcene loved to eat just about anything.

As the conversation with Arcene was interrupted by Letje, and he knew that part of the game was over, Artek found his heart beating faster and a smile spreading across his face. Soon she would arrive, then his rule could begin in earnest.

One thing Artek had no knowledge of was the return of Marcus, a man believed dead to the whole world apart from a few that had discovered the original him deep within The Commorancy.

~~~

Artek admired himself in the mirror, nodding in satisfaction. Hair was perfect, trimmed meticulously, then brushed carefully so that not a strand was out of place. His shirt was an emerald green that shone as it caught the light creeping in through the rather small, high window, and his slender frame was the perfect hangar for his trademark three quarter length coat.

Uncharacteristically, he fumbled with a button nervously, then checked the bank of monitors located along the wall in his day room. He walked over and peered closely at one screen in particular, smiling at the sight that greeted him.

She's here, she's here. Shame about the man though, but no matter, he won't be a problem. And Letje too, this should be interesting, very interesting indeed.

There was a knock at the door before his mother entered, hair just as perfect, attire spotless, dour look on her face like it was the only facial expression she now was capable of showing.

"Well, let's go get this over with then," said Malessa, turning then haughtily leaving the room.

"Yes Mother."

Won't be long now, and you, my dear mother, will be surplus to requirements. I'll have my Arcene and the country to rule over. That's a start at least.

With a final glance in the mirror, Artek pressed a button on a bank full of similar looking buttons, switches, roller-balls and knobs, and the monitors flickered then went dark.

I'm coming my Queen.

She Wouldn't. Would She?

"What do you mean she'll get captured?" Fasolt stared into Marcus' swirling eyes, pulsing like a strobe light as they continued their conversation.

"I mean exactly that: she'll get captured. My bet would be that she does it voluntarily, without telling the others. But if not then Artek, and whoever he has working for him, will capture them, all of them."

"Then why would you send them out? It seemed so odd that you would allow them to go without either you or me, or both of us going along."

Marcus stared at Fasolt, waiting to see if he would come to his own conclusion. The silence stretched out until he had no choice but to break it himself. "Fasolt, you have been here now for what, five years? Yes?"

"Yes. A little more, but I don't really keep track."

"So you are more than aware of just what this place has to offer? What it can do to people? For people?" Fasolt just nodded so Marcus continued. "And you know just how bad it is out there in the rest of the country don't you? How bad it has been right since the start. Right since The Lethargy began and your son made things so much worse with his 'religion'. It's always been hit and miss — the future of us, of us all. It's always been so precarious, so delicate a balance of births as opposed to deaths.

"Many have found it strange, if not totally unfair that I have made entry to The Commorancy so convoluted and difficult, as if I didn't really want just your average person to come, to Awaken, to stand a chance in this terrible new world we find ourselves living through, but that has never been the case at all. I want more than anything for people to make it through to the other side, but the problem is that there is no other side. The Lethargy will always be here, will always remain as long as there are just ordinary people. Whole people often give birth to children with Lethargy, or they develop it at some point. Where do you think that leads?"

Fasolt was beginning to understand the true depth of Marcus, and marveled at the long term approach he had obviously taken, right from the beginning. "You had a plan, right from the start, didn't you?"

Marcus nodded, his hair bobbing along, eyes smiling through the higher end of the spectrum. "I did. There is always a plan Fasolt, always. I made it difficult to gain entry to The Commorancy exactly so that it would only be those with the drive, with the ambition, the fortitude, to ever have the chance to take advantage of what it has to offer."

"You're talking about natural selection, that's kind of..."

"Extreme?"

Fasolt nodded, his hair banging on the table, almost knocking over his cup of tea.

"If that's what it was then I would agree. But the fact of the matter is that I know things nobody else knows. Whole? People who don't get The Lethargy? Well, some of them have it, some of them are guaranteed to either have it as they age, or to definitely pass it on to their children. They may not go into the kind of stupors that those with true Lethargy or The Creeping do, but it subdues them, stops them wanting things, doing things for themselves. It makes them static. Those people would never really try to obtain entry here. It takes real people, truly Whole people who want something out of life to get here.

"And although the rumors of just how hard it is to gain entry have become myth over the years, the actual truth is that it is very easy, if you try. All it takes is a little bit of drive and ambition, or merely to be truly Whole and want to make a go of it. If you try for a while then you will get a Room. Even if you give up, the chances are that I will personally offer you an invitation. I have done it a number of times over the years."

"How do you know this Marcus? About Whole not truly being Whole?"

Marcus sighed. "Fasolt, you are a very powerful man, probably one of the most powerful there has ever been, but do you not understand it yet? I see it, I see it all. It drives me mad. I live a life already lived a million, a trillion times with countless tiny convergences. I see them all, these lives; I can reach out and grasp them, pull them into my mind through The Noise, and I know. I know so much and I can do so much, but I cannot change what The Lethargy has done to people, I can only try to find a way through what is almost an infinitely impossible maze and hope, even pray, that somehow we manage to come out the other side as a race that thrives on this planet we call home."

Fasolt said nothing; Marcus could see that he understood. To a degree he probably understood more than any other person ever could, apart from Letje if she managed to do what Marcus expected she would, or at least thought she had a small chance, on one timeline at least, of accomplishing.

Marcus continued. "We won't make it unless we go past what we think of as Whole, it simply isn't working. I knew it from the very first day that I truly Awoke and saw The Noise in all its infinite glory. Did you know I have even visited The Void?" Fasolt shook again, lost in the words of Marcus Wolfe. "I see the lives spread out before you, before everyone I have met. Lives lived, to be lived, all jumbled up into a confusion of pasts and presents — such things mean nothing in The Void. I see countless species in the Universe. All of them come from there, you know? We are all but dust, not even that important, and however long we live it will come to an end one day, and we will be reborn, maybe in the future, or in the past, it's all the same in there, and none of it means anything more than that The Void endures. The energy lasts forever, it merely changes form. We mean so little and we mean so much. Nothing and everything.

"So I saw from the start that something had to be done, so I built The Commorancy. I am quite sure it has driven me mad in its own way, changed me too much to be seen as just a man any longer, but I think that this madness is the new sane for those of us that Awaken. And we need to Fasolt, people must take control of their lives and their bodies and learn how to live longer, populate the planet with children that will Awaken. They need to live longer so they have ample time to find the right person for them. There are so few that it takes so much more time to find a partner than it ever did when we were but children. But if just a few manage to stay alive, slowly, ever so slowly rebuild, then it will happen one day: humanity will thrive once again in a way I don't think you or even I could ever truly imagine."

"And Letje, what does this have to do with her? And you still have not answered why you sent her out without our protection, knowing that she would either be captured or allow herself to be. What reasoning is there for this act?"

"Because, Fasolt, we need to protect The Commorancy. That part of what I said was the reason is true. I left it before and I shouldn't have, but I had my reasons. The other Marcus' had their reasons in any case. But it could cope for a while on its own, I have no doubt. No, the truth is that Letje is the answer to everything, so she must face this challenge herself and deal with it herself."

"But why? She has help in any case. Gamm is a strange one, and more powerful than he knows."

"I know; I like him. But if Letje is to solve this stealing of people, of putting our very future at risk, all of our futures, then she must go to the man who is doing it and she must end it, return people to their rightful place in the world — or The Void — and know that it was her, not us, or me, or anyone else, that saved everything. Everyone."

"But why? I still don't understand."

"Isn't it obvious? So she can be Queen. Rule the whole of civilization. Take control of the entire planet, be a Goddess, a woman fearsome and incredibly powerful: the Saviour of humanity. The Mother Goddess that people will look to for guidance, follow with their very souls until such time as Letje finally passes to dust at some point far, far, far into a future I am no longer a part of and unable to see."

"And how far into the future might that be Marcus?"

"Oh, let's just say it's rather a long time and leave it at that. But the chances are that none of that will come to pass Fasolt, and there are infinite paths she might take that lead somewhere else for us all. Even this path that I do hope she follows is so remote in terms of succeeding that I really do fear for the future of us all. It could all be over very soon Fasolt, a few generations if this Artek succeeds. He is a child, a boy, he has no idea what he is doing. If he did then he wouldn't be doing what he is." Marcus leaned back in his chair, arms folded behind his head. "In any case, we shall see. And we may as well enjoy life while we can. Whatever happens, I get the feeling that you and I won't be going anywhere any time soon. We have long lives ahead of us. At least, we might. Tea?"

"Eh?"

Marcus knew he had said a lot, but he had been locked up alone for so long that he found it such a relief to talk to somebody and to share the burden, even if it was with a man who had not so very long ago conspired to destroy everything that he had gone to such pains to build. But he hadn't understood the consequences of his actions, not really, not deep down in his soul. And besides, Marcus had won. "Tea? Do you want a cup of tea?"

"Oh, yes please. I think I need it."

Beautiful Skin

Marcus always enjoyed these moments, although if he thought about it then this was the first time he personally had ever performed such an act. He'd done it countless times, opened countless doors, welcomed no end of people to the world once more after their time in their Room, yet here he was, somehow feeling nervous about welcoming a man called Edsel who should be turning the handle on the door marked EXIT right about... now.

"Hello Edsel, I'm Marcus."

"Um, hi Marcus. We have met before you know?"

"Yes, yes, of course we have. Haha, just being polite. But, well, things have changed somewhat since you entered your Room, so don't be surprised if you hear some rather strange rumors once you are back out there in the wider world."

"Rumors? What kind of rumors?"

"Well, nothing to concern yourself with for now. Let's just say that currently The Commorancy is under new ownership: a woman named Letje. She's very nice, you may get to meet her one day, but I'm back now, after some, shall we say, rather heady times, and you can rest assured that soon it will be business as usual. But I digress, none of that means anything to you, and we have more important things to discuss at any rate."

Edsel was clearly confused by such talk immediately after the time in his Room was up, and Marcus realized his error. "Sorry, too much information. Don't you worry about it, the most important thing is that you got what you came for, yes?"

"Oh yes, I can't thank you enough Marcus, I really can't. Look at me, my beautiful skin." Edsel held his arms out parallel to the floor, twirling and smiling like he'd been reborn. "It's not finished, but I've been doing as you said, working hard on my body, changing things as slowly as I dared. Although I have to say it was almost impossible not to just try to make it all happen at once."

"Better to take it slow and make sure the job is done right," said Marcus, smiling, happy that Edsel had truly Awoken and had followed the instructions he'd been given before entering his Room. Edsel was a special case, a man who had endured no end of suffering over many years, a man who was eighteen when The Lethargy took hold, living through some of the worst periods of post-Lethargy Britain, when mania seized and Varik and his church were rising just as The Commorancy was.

"Absolutely," agreed Edsel. "For the first time in I don't know how many years I actually enjoy looking in the mirror again. It's like I hadn't seen myself for so long, dared not to look."

"Well, I for one quite liked it. The blue at any rate."

"So you said, a few others have as well. But it was too much of a reminder, of what happened, of bad decisions, of loss and the lies I told myself, the lies told to me. All just the perils of having been born when I was born I guess, but I can't tell you how free I feel."

"Well I'm very glad for you Edsel, I truly am. Keep taking it slow, let the skin do what it has to do in its own time, and very soon you will been as perfect as a newborn."

Edsel listened carefully, being the good student that he had been before he entered. He may have truly Awoken, come out of his Room with countless centuries of life ahead of him if he so wished, but above all he wanted to ensure that he knew exactly how to eradicate the countless reminders of terrible events that had left his skin stained, blistered, scarred and ruined from the tips of his toes to the top of his head. This was why he had applied for a Room, and he was a man that was not one to waste opportunities.

"Marcus, I can't tell you how much this means to me, but I do have a question. But, hey, what happened to your eyes?"

"It's rather a long story I'm afraid, and I have some pressing matters to attend to, but if you would like to stay in The Room For Guests then I can talk to you soon about what has happened while you have been otherwise occupied."

"Okay, that sounds marvelous. Just a day or two though, and that's what I wanted to ask you about. How long has it been Marcus? Days drifted into a dream in my Room, time felt different, but I know it has been some time. What I want to know is how are the others?"

There were things to tell Edsel, things that would have to wait just a little longer. There was no point telling him too much too soon, it was better for him to become a little adjusted to life outside of his Room first. "Please, follow me, let's walk while we talk."

They walked down the living corridor, birds peeking out from the safety of the walls, watching as the two men passed by before resuming their chatter.

"So, my family?"

"You have to understand that you have been here for many, many years Edsel. A very long time indeed. A lot has happened out in the world, a lot has happened here in The Commorancy too, so you will find yourself in a very different place to the one you left behind so long ago."

"How long has it been?"

"A while," said Marcus cryptically. "Quite a while."

"Ten years? Twenty? Thirty?"

"A little over seventy five years Edsel, that's how long you have been in your Room."

"Wow, it sure went fast. It doesn't surprise me though, not much would anymore."

"Well, I'm glad to hear it. You know, you were lucky. When you arrived you had already lived far longer than almost anyone who hadn't come here to Awaken, so you understood that you could live a long time. It means it's not quite such a shock when you hear how extended your stay here has been."

"Yeah, there is Awakening and there is Commorancy Awakening though. Right? It's been different here, I've learned so much, I don't know how you devise Rooms to do such things, Awaken things I never even thought of inside of me, but it worked, and I won't let you down."

"My dear Edsel, you don't owe me a thing. Just live your life the best way you possibly can."

"I will. And Marcus, the others, how are they?"

"Come, let's have something to eat, then I'll tell you all about it."

Edsel walked beside Marcus, and Marcus knew that this was one man that more than deserved his Room and the gifts it gave him — some people were simply owed what he could offer, Edsel was certainly one of them. Now he just had to discuss the matter of his family with him. Marcus didn't know whether Edsel would laugh or cry at such news, but there was no doubt that he now had the knowledge inside of him to be able to do what needed to be done to be re-united with them once more, however long it actually took.

At least this is one family that won't have just disappeared. Where there is life there is hope.

Marcus turned and looked at Edsel. "Um, Edsel, would you mind awfully if we made a stop at The Room For Clothes?"

"Sure, you want to get changed?"

"No, actually I don't. It's just, well, I think it would be better if we actually got you dressed, don't you? I know you are pleased with the way you are looking now, but well, I'm not so sure that it is the best way to go back out into the world, are you?"

Edsel stared down at his naked torso and smiled. "Oh, yeah, right. Sorry Marcus, it's just that I've hated looking at myself for so long, it kind of became novel to watch my skin coming back to life, you know."

"I know. Trust me, I understand completely."

Marcus led Edsel down the corridor, which closed up behind them, the dream of the Room forgotten already by the impossible sentience that by now had moved on to dreaming of other things more important than the wishes of a single solitary man. However important he may have felt himself to be, it meant nothing on the scale of things. Nothing whatsoever.

At the Gates

Letje felt like a fraud, but what other choice was there? She looked at Gamm and Arcene, careful to hide any hint of her deception from them. Was she doing the right thing? Would they hate her forever for what she was setting in motion? Or would they thank her in the end?

Did it matter? It was her decision to make, it was her that led this group, had the final say. It went unsaid, but each of them understood that Letje was the power behind the direction their lives would take, that of the rest of the country too, not to mention her being the absolute ruler of the most important source of protecting the future of humanity — The Commorancy.

So Letje kept her emotions in check, stood tall and strong, smiled at her friends even as she felt like what she was doing was betraying their trust in her.

She even felt guilty about misleading Leel. The crazy dog was sat there beside Arcene, looking expectantly at the gates just like the rest of them were.

Letje still couldn't quite get used to the fact that Leel was just a dog — she was more like a small horse in size. Sat down with her head held high, Leel was practically as tall as Arcene. It still seemed incredible that such a large creature was basically nothing more than a juvenile, and would be forever, never tiring of playing, running, and eating. *Just like Arcene really. There couldn't be a better match for two friends, surely?* Letje smiled at the thought of just how well suited they were for each other, then turned her head back to the front, just as the others were doing so intently.

They were stood at the outer gates to the prison. Curving across the entry in elaborate script was a large, decorative sign that read Bridewell, rather at odds with the stark lines of the rest of the purely functional gates and the building that could be seen through rows of wire mesh topped with barbed wire and impossibly high.

Arcene pressed the buzzer again on the gun-metal gray box attached neatly to the brick wall that spread out for a quarter mile either side of the gate — a recent addition as far as Letje could tell. Very recent. Arcene pressed it again, peering into the curved dome that was obviously a camera.

"Stop that," hissed Letje. "They know we're here, no need to keep pressing the buzzer."

Arcene whipped her head to the side, hair flying about dramatically. *She's doing that on purpose, she thinks she's the star in a story.*

"Well why don't they come and open the gates then? This is stupid. And I still don't see how this is a good idea anyway. Neither does Leel. Do you Leel?"

Leel let out a loud woof, getting a nice scratch behind the ear from Arcene in return for being a good girl.

"I already told you, I know how this Artek's mind works. He's not going to just take us, he wouldn't dare. And now we know what he can do, what he did to Marcus, well, I can stop him from doing it to us."

"I'm inclined to agree with Arcene on this Letje. It simply doesn't seem like a very good idea at all."

"We won't go in, promise. Just have a chat, see what this man is really like, then we'll leave. At least then we will all know where we stand. Hey, here they come." Letje stared through the bars at the sight of Artek casually approaching, a woman that was clearly a relation beside him — their style and features almost exact copies apart from the male/female difference. That was it, no hordes of kidnappers, no army of men wielding all manner of scary weapons, just a man and a woman slowly walking toward them.

As they got closer, Letje had the chance to inspect them before they arrived, and it was already clear that the woman had an extreme dislike for them all, particularly Arcene, if the terrible looks she was giving her were anything to go by. But there was something about her, the same as there was about Artek: like they thought they were better than other people, that they had some kind of a right to the world they walked in, that it owed them, and they would take it, take what they felt they were due, certainly never saying thank you for it either. Letje could read them by the way they walked, some kind of inner confidence that definitely went beyond just bordering on arrogance and was pretty much contempt for everything apart from themselves — especially the woman, she was clearly one tough lady, and judging by the way her face remained impassive she wasn't that keen on smiling.

The man Artek, if this was him, and Letje was sure it was, had a much less solemn expression. He was smiling like a cat that had a mouse cornered, his grin getting wider and wider the closer he got to them. No, not them, Arcene — he only had eyes for Arcene.

"So beautiful. More beautiful than anything I have ever seen in my entire life. I am honored Arcene, truly honored."

Is she blushing? She is, she's actually blushing. Oh dear, this isn't going to go as planned.

Arcene was practically glowing, reaching her hand through the bars and allowing Artek to kiss it gently while the woman glowered, looking like she was attempting to set Arcene ablaze through the intensity of her stare alone.

"Do you think so? Really?"

Oh dear, I think I need to calm this situation down.

Letje coughed politely, waiting to see just what manners the man and woman really had.

127

"Oh, do excuse my son," *Ah, so that's it! How old is she then?* "I'm afraid he seems to have lost his manners. Allow me to introduce myself. I am Malessa, and this is my son Artek, Artek Ligertwood." Malessa extended her hand through the bars, where Artek was still holding on to Arcene's.

Gamm reached forward first and introduced himself, holding his hand out for Artek, who reluctantly let go of Arcene and shook Gamm's hand perfunctorily, paying him absolutely no attention. Letje wasn't given much more than a quick glance either, before Artek returned his gaze to Arcene.

"And you, I know you my dear. You are Arcene," said Malessa.

It was as if Arcene came out of a daze and realized where she was and just what kind of girl she was.

The spell's broken, for now, thought Letje.

"Huh? Oh, yes, I'm Arcene. How do you do."

Did she just curtsy!

"Very well my dear, and my son is certainly a lot better for finally meeting you."

Arcene stared back at Artek, head tilting from side to side, clearly curious about the strange looking man. "You're Devan then? The man that got me into so much trouble?" Arcene pouted, red full lips that Artek was practically salivating over.

"I'm afraid I am. I do hope that I can be forgiven for my deception, but I simply had to find a way to get to know you. So when the opportunity arose I'm afraid that I took it. I apologize if you got into trouble though, and nothing bad happened?" He scowled deeply at Letje, the look promising untold hurt if she had harmed the woman he was evidently besotted with.

I can't believe we missed this, it's the most important piece of information we now have. That and his mother is still alive. He'd told Marcus she was dead.

It was clear that his mother had a strong influence over Artek, and it was also more than evident that she held the rest of them in contempt. Certainly Arcene was not worthy of her son, that much was obvious; Artek didn't seem bothered in the least.

There's something going on there, he's not worried by what his mother thinks.

Arcene answered Artek's question with a shrug. "Nothing too bad happened, but I did get told off and we all had to change our passwords."

"Well, sorry once again. Now, why don't you all come inside and we can get to know each other better?"

"I don't think we will be doing that just yet," said Gamm, stepping forward as if it was imperative he put himself between the two women he was with and Artek. "We just came to say hello, and to let you know that we found you. But for now we shall say our goodbyes. I'm sure we will meet again soon enough."

"As you wish," said Artek, turning to Letje and Arcene, asking, "Is this what you ladies want? I do hope you aren't being forced to act in a way that you would rather be different. You are more than welcome to come inside."

"Um, no, we're fine," said Arcene. "Just popping along to say hey, but we have to go now, don't we Letje?"

"We do, but we'll meet again. Goodbye."

"We certainly will meet again, and goodbye Arcene, it was so lovely to meet you in person," said Artek.

"Um, yeah, you too. Come on Leel."

They walked away, the strange atmosphere dissipating once they made their way back into the countryside that surrounded Bridewell.

They kept walking and didn't stop for an hour. Nobody spoke a word, which really put Letje on edge — Arcene couldn't keep quiet for five minutes normally, even if her life depended on it.

~~~

"I don't like him," said Arcene in a sulk. "Why did we have to go and meet them like that? Why bother?"

"Well, what other option is there? Let them just find us and take us, without us having met them and at least learned some valuable information?"

"Like what?"

"Like the fact that Artek is clearly besotted with you, and that he's been chasing you, watching you, for years. You almost fell for him too, I could see it."

Arcene was on her feet, Leel jumping up quickly, wondering what they were going to be doing. "I did no such thing Letje, you take that back. Ugh, I don't want anything to do with boys, no offense Gamm. But, well, I did feel a little funny when we first met him, like I wasn't quite myself. I had this weird picture in my head of wearing a crown full of shining jewels and some big dress that swept down across the ground, with him standing beside me with his silly hair and... Dunno, it was weird."

"That's why I wanted us to meet him. Them. We learned he has a very powerful mother that is clearly a big influence, know he's in love with you—" Arcene interrupted with a snort, "and is very powerful in The Noise. I could feel him trying to do things, trying to make us forget what we were doing there, forget that we were even talking to him, and he was going to open the gates and take us inside. All of that is valuable information."

"It was a risk though Letje, a huge risk."

"I know, but we have to start this. We have to know a little of what we are up against, and that was about the best I could come up with. It was that or simply wait until they bothered to come out to find us somewhere, and that certainly wouldn't have gone as well as that meeting just did. Remember, this man, or more likely, him and his mother and some other help, have been taking people for who knows how long. Not only that, they have been taking my friends, people that

I bet are inside that horrible building right now, maybe not even knowing that they are actually prisoners."

"He didn't say hello to Leel."

"What?"

"Artek, Devan, whatever," said Arcene, waving a hand dismissively. "He didn't say hello to Leel, he just ignored her totally. That says a lot."

"Hmm, maybe you're right Arcene, who knows? Not everyone loves dogs, certainly not as much as you do, that's for sure."

"Everyone that's nice loves dogs. Look at her, she's beautiful." Arcene rubbed a knuckle over Leel's head; she squirmed with joy.

"Will you be careful!"

Arcene was moving about too much, forgetting again about the sword that she had in her hand — even sheathed she could do some serious damage.

"Oops, sorry. Anyway, what's the plan now?" Arcene stared at Letje accusingly, as if everything that had happened was her fault, not in some part Arcene's for the information she had supplied to Artek.

"Well, now that you happen to ask."

Hide and Seek

"What do you mean we're going to run?" Gamm stopped poking the fire, a pathetic small thing, but burning fiercely hot, not a wisp of smoke giving away a hint as to their location.

"I mean that we know a little of what they want. It's obvious just by where they are that they have people imprisoned in that building, that's what it is after all. We also know that they, well, Artek, wants Arcene. So we should run."

Should I be playing with them like this? Is it fair? But they aren't just going to let themselves be captured, are they?

Letje knew there was nothing for it but to be captured if they were to get inside so they could try to stop Artek and his mother from doing what they were doing. She also understood that the risk was enormous — not only to her, but to everyone else in the country too. There were a few hints of people's lifeforce visible inside the sprawling complex of the prison now known as Bridewell, but most of it was blocked to her — Artek and his mother were powerful, there was no mistaking that. The only answer was to infiltrate the place, and the more Letje had tried to formulate a plan as they got closer, the more she came to realize that this was exactly what Marcus had wanted to happen: he knew they would be captured, expected it.

If that was the best that he could come up with, a man that understood the world they lived in better than any other human being, at least in terms of what was possible for The Awoken, then she doubted very much she would come up with something better herself.

"We should leave and see what happens, see what they do. There is no way we are going to get inside and save everyone. You have seen the place right? I can guarantee there will be traps and there will be measures put in place to make certain that nobody leaves unless they want them to. So we should leave and see what they do. Maybe Artek will come out after us, after Arcene anyway, and we can deal with him when he's alone."

"That's stupid," was all Arcene had to say on the matter. She was itching for a fight and the more 'deathy' she'd got along the way the more her bloodlust seemed to rise.

"Letje, this is making no sense. We came to find them and now we have, so we need to formulate some kind of a plan so we can get inside, try to save everyone. What else is there? We have no army, no reinforcements, there are no people now, just us and whoever is left inside. So we need to make that our goal.

Maybe if they are aware of the decision then it will work better? No, if I tell them then Artek or his mother will know too, and then they might act totally differently. They will know I am powerful if I have got us captured on purpose.

The only problem was the deception: she hated lying to Arcene and Gamm.

Letje came to a decision.

"Alright, I'm sorry, but I have to tell you something. And you're not going to like it."

~~~

"You lied! Traitor. How come it's alright for you but when I do something then you put me on trial? It's not fair." Arcene was livid, stomping about like she'd been grounded until she was at least three hundred, constantly turning and letting more accusations fly at Letje — who hadn't been able to get a word in since she admitted her treachery.

"Maybe we should give Letje the chance to explain herself Arcene? And can you please tell your dog that my leg is not a toy and that I rather like wearing my own boots and they are in no way designed to be eaten?" Gamm shook his leg, trying to get Leel to release her hold on his boot, a boot that fit easily into her mouth and that she had developed a real taste for.

"Fine. Leel, bad girl, you let go."

Leel dropped her tail low and released her grip, skulking back over to Arcene where she instantly perked up as she got a pat on the head for being a good girl. Suddenly she was occupied by a very exciting stick and lay down tearing at it contentedly.

"Thank you Gamm. Now, I'm sorry okay? As I said, I couldn't, can't, see any other way, and I'm sure that this is what Marcus knew would happen too. We have to get inside and we have to then find a way to save everyone."

"That's no reason to lie. Lying is bad, bad, bad."

"I know, but this is important. More important than any of us. It's the future of everything."

"Well what is the plan then?" asked Arcene, sitting and trying to pull the wedge of stick out of Leel's mouth where she'd trapped it sideways, her jaw craned wide open. "Stupid dog," she muttered.

"The plan is that we get inside, let them take us, and then we stop them."

"That's not much of a plan Letje," said Gamm.

"No, but they won't know that we've let them take us, will they? Will they Arcene?" Letje stared at her sternly, knowing that Arcene did rather like to talk, and wasn't the best at keeping secrets. Not that Letje could say she was much better at the moment.

"Hey, why pick on me? Gamm could be a right old blabbermouth for all we know."

"I'm not," said Gamm, offended.

"So let's leave like I said, and wait for them to come and capture us."

"Then what? Ah, got it, don't do that again Leel. Silly girl."

"Then once we are inside we will know that they know we know, and they will know that we know they know."

"Huh?"

"I'm with her, I don't get it."

"It's a game, it always has been. They are playing theirs and we are playing ours." Letje didn't know how to put it better than that.

"So are you saying that they will know that we wanted to be captured? If so then what's the point? Why not just walk up there now and ask them to open the doors?" Gamm looked confused, and rightly so.

"Because Artek and his mother are going to think that when we just met them they managed to influence us and think that they messed with our heads, that's why. They will think that we've forgotten all about them, but we haven't. Have we?"

"Forgotten about who?" asked Arcene.

"What are we talking about again?" asked Gamm.

Oh no, not already. I was sure I stopped them from making us forget.

"Haha, got you," said Arcene.

Gamm just smiled guiltily. "Sorry, I couldn't resist either."

"You nearly gave me a heart attack. So you do remember?"

"Of course we do," said Gamm. Arcene just nodded, smiling happily at fooling Letje.

"One thing though," said Gamm. "I still don't get it. As soon as they capture us then it isn't going to make any difference how we got inside, whether they think we remember them or not. Is it?"

"It is. It shows that we can't be fooled; it shows that he's not able to do it to everyone, not if I'm there anyway. And it shows that we are better than them."

Gamm didn't get it in the slightest, and the more Letje thought about it the less any of it made sense even to her.

~~~

"Did it work?" asked Malessa.

"Mother! Of course it did. They won't have a clue what they are doing; they will be as confused as newborns, thinking they have some kind of a plan, that they could resist my influence. They just don't understand what they are dealing with. I wonder if even you do Mother." Artek looked into his mother's cold eyes, defying her, not looking away.

"And you, my son, underestimate me. Now, tell me what you did." Malessa waited as Artek continued his staring. "Please."

"I could feel that Letje was powerful, no doubt about it. Probably the most powerful woman I have ever met, and yes, that includes you. But she already had a plan, one she was going to keep secret from the others. Stupid really, as all it involved was getting captured, making us think that we had the upper hand."

"Well, we do, don't we?"

"Absolutely. I just kind of mixed it up a little, so they will allow us to 'capture' them, but she thinks she can resist my influence, she thinks she has the better of me." Artek stopped and thought for a minute. "It's all kind of pointless really. If Letje was to allow them to be captured then I don't know what she is playing at making it something she keeps from the others. No matter, she will tell them, they will all be confused, we will have them soon enough. And Arcene, did you see her? How beautiful."

"Yet far from elegant," said Malessa in disgust. "She's worse than the nuns — a savage."

Artek's face turned as red as his hair. "I've told you before," he spat, "do not talk of her like that. Ever." Artek left the room. He had plans to bring to fruition; his Queen would be with him soon.

Lost Friends

Letje knew that parts of her were missing, as if The Lethargy had taken hold, stripping her of access to segments of her mind — memories and experiences locked behind closed doors, the key out of reach.

She was happy though, sort of, yet knew that it wasn't right, that there were things she should remember, things she was supposed to know, and do, yet she couldn't quite bring them to memory, found she was unable to act as she didn't know what she was supposed to be trying to accomplish.

Locked up for extended periods in the selection of rooms that were their quarters, she knew that it wasn't right, that she really should object, but there didn't seem to be any reason why. Life was good, there were routines, things were alright. Weren't they?

They were there, the memories, just below the surface, waiting to be grabbed hold of, to allow life to make sense, for events to fall into order and reveal their true meaning.

Letje felt like she was in a daze, able to think clearly yet with a cloud hanging over her, obscuring the truth of her reality, yet try as she might she just couldn't quite grab hold of the tenuous threads that would link it all together.

She was wandering the halls, footsteps echoing down the empty corridors, roaming the place she now called home, knowing that she had done such things before, knowing that she wasn't really supposed to be allowed yet for some reason today she was able to leave her quarters, the door unlocked, to wander the dark and depressing place that had row after row of cells, most doors open, empty, nothing but ghosts remaining.

A happy tune was whistled as she wandered aimlessly, yet at the same time she knew it was a fake happiness, only going so deep, not a true reflection of her state of mind, somehow forced yet she was unable to care.

Things were wrong; things were how they were meant to be.

The steel thudded dully as she ran a hand along the bars to the cell doors as she passed, but then she stopped. A face, a beautiful face, shone out from the gloom of a small room containing little more than a bed, a wooden chair, and a table with assorted creams, lotions and the usual items found at a ladies dresser.

"Letje?" said Umeko, "Is that you?"

"Huh?" Letje stared at the features of the woman that had spoken, a countenance that was almost

141

radiant, hinting at a beauty that would shine out fiercely if the woman was living a life that would make her happy. Have children, a husband, the things she had always wanted more than anything else. Her skin was like the color of a plum...

"Umeko? Umeko, it's you!"

Everything came flooding back, memories of Umeko, of a warm day when she stood in the middle of an overgrown road and watched as Umeko met a man, her joy ringing out into the air at the realization she had found the husband that would allow her to bear children.

That was merely the tip of the iceberg. Memories poured into her mind, the reality of her situation slamming into her like a cell door closing on her memory loss. How could she have allowed this to happen? How could she have been so easy to fool? To be living a life under lock and key when she was meant to be saving everyone, finding a solution to the problem?

This was the risk she had taken; the realization that she had failed was hard to take.

How could she have been living in what amounted to a cell herself, although it was well-appointed and luxurious, sharing the space with Arcene who Artek was besotted with? How long had it been now? Months, it had been months, and memories of her feeling convinced at being able to overcome the power of Artek came back to her, the feeling that she would be more than a match for the man, confident she would find a way to stop him and his insane quest to empty the country, subjugate an already much diminished population.

Now Umeko. Had she met her here before? No, she would remember, but she recalled in vivid detail seeing others in similar situations: Stanley, Kirstie and other people, staring at her from behind bars, pleading for help or lost in a haze of forgetfulness.

"Can you get me out," whispered Umeko, poking her head between the bars as much as she could, staring up and down the corridor anxiously. "You have to help me. This place isn't right, everything's wrong."

"I will, don't worry. I'll get you out."

Letje felt like a fool, to have been taken so easily, to have been defenseless like a child, when she should have been able to tear apart the mind of the man at the heart of the problem.

"Ah, there you are," said Artek, walking toward her calmly, feet tapping on the dull concrete floor. "I do apologize, you weren't supposed to be out here you know Letje?" he chided. "But no matter, there is no harm done."

Letje felt herself slipping, felt the past wrap her in a warm, fuzzy embrace. Everything was good, she was happy, she wanted to go back to her quarters and check on Arcene.

Artek led the way. Letje followed, whistling a happy tune as she went.

It had happened before, a number of similar meetings. It didn't matter, Artek always found her eventually.

Defiance

"You dare to do such a thing without me agreeing? You have no right." Artek was angrier than he had ever been with his mother, and he had been plenty angry with her plenty of times.

Malessa stood proud and erect. "I had every right, and besides, they were disgusting," she answered defiantly.

"Well I liked them, they would have come in useful, and they knew things. We could have found out so much more from them, now we can't."

"They were useless. Just stupid little ugly creatures that were eating our food and taking up time that could be better spent elsewhere. I made the decision and now it's done."

Artek got up close to his mother, grabbing her by her bare shoulders, the tight fitting green dress sitting just perfectly across her chest. "They were mine. I brought them here, just like I did nearly everyone else, and I," Artek pointed at his chest, "decide who gets to

145

stay and who doesn't. Not you." He jabbed his mother hard just beneath the collar bone and she staggered back in shock.

"You dare to assault me? Your own mother? No son of mine was ever brought up to be so disrespectful. Mind your manners child, or there will be consequences."

"Ha, I think not Mother. Those days are long gone. I am a man and I will not be treated like a boy." Artek stormed out of the room, slamming the door behind him.

Just like a child, thought Malessa, smiling. Glad that she had finally got her way, even if it did annoy her son. He'd be fine though, in a day or two he would have calmed down. Her decision had been for the best — she couldn't stand to look at those vile creatures. Just knowing they were there was enough to turn her off her food.

~~~

Artek walked out into the huge courtyard accessed from quadrant 5 of Bridewell, the place where the bodies were dealt with. He turned up his nose at the smell, but had to make sure that what he had been told by that horrible guard Victor really was true. He knew it was; he went to look anyway.

He wasn't disgusted by the sight of death, he had seen too much of it, dealt out so much of it, that it didn't touch him. Usually it made him happy, as it meant the world was a little cleaner of sub-species that would be no use in the future rule of his family through the ages — they had to begin with only the best possible subjects to create a new world full of perfection.

The smell though, that was always an issue — the assault on his nostrils always seemed to come as a surprise. The bodies had only been out for a day but already they were fairly ripe. The warm weather meant insects had gathered in the thousands, and the bloated bodies gave off gases that reached even where he stood, well away from the huge pile.

For such small people they actually made quite a funeral pyre. The men, women, and even the children, although it was hard to tell the difference as they were all about the same size, were piled haphazardly on top of each other in the huge pit, arms and legs in positions impossible in life. It seemed that Victor hadn't even wanted to waste bullets, so the bodies were badly damaged. No respectful mercy killing was this, it was brutal and uncalled for. Something would have to be done about his mother's chosen aide.

The pile was a mix of faded nun's habits, bloodied garments and obvious signs of barbaric beatings about the heads, now swollen to an even more grotesque degree than they had been in life. Finally throats had been slit, and by the looks if it Victor had flung many of them onto the pile while still alive, letting them bleed out while they lay atop the dead and the dying of their strange small community.

He'd had high hopes for The Sisters — much as he hated to look at them with their huge heads and sharp teeth Artek knew that they held secrets, had powers and knowledge that would be invaluable for the security of his family's future. They knew things nobody else did, and now they had taken some of that knowledge to the grave with them. Artek moved over to the pile of mangled bodies, walking around it, looking for something.

Just in case, just to be sure his mother wasn't up to anything else.

No, there she was. Mother Superior, eyes defiant even in death, her nun's habit torn and bloody. Her cornette was off her head, revealing her strange hair and the extent of the beating she had been given before her throat had been cut. She was covered in her own blood and Artek could see the trail of it leading down over her Sisters and the few men they had always thought of as second class citizens. Well, they were all equal now. Death — always the great equalizer.

Bad Choices

It had now been four months, and Artek had to admit that he was getting somewhat frustrated with the situation he found himself in — a situation he had brought to fruition so he had nobody to blame but himself, and his mother of course.

She was getting too much, her domineering behavior was escalating to levels he had never seen before, and he found it increasingly tiresome to be in her presence. Didn't she know he had other things on his mind? He had a child growing inside of Arcene, a little baby boy that was to be his son and heir, and however much he was regretting the infatuation he had with the uncouth child — for that was all he could think of her as, certainly not a lady, a woman, and definitely no Queen, he was sorry to admit — she would certainly not be 'got rid of' as his mother put it.

Arcene was, when all was said and done, entirely too willful. When left to her own devices, something he had to do on a regular basis as he was unsure what effect it would have on the still-forming child if he kept her constantly unaware of her situation and what was happening, Arcene was almost entirely out of control. Artek couldn't understand how she had so much energy, why she loved that stupid dog he dare not get rid off in case she became so distraught she lost the child, and he simply failed to understand why she refused to even try to act in the correct manner.

It was frustrating beyond belief and he became more exasperated by the day. After months in her company, and with the child growing inside of her, she was showing absolutely no sign of slowing down, accepting what was happening, or giving him the least bit of the recognition that he clearly deserved. She had no recollection of their pairing most of the time, and it was something Artek himself wished he could forget. He had kept her mindless enough so that there was no struggle when they lay together, but she was still almost impossible to control — she acted like a wild animal, like he was committing a heinous crime, and Artek found the whole encounter entirely unsatisfying.

When all was said and done it was like taking advantage of a child — not what he had expected at all. Arcene was not curvaceous and womanly as he had imagined her to be now she was a little older. He thought she would have grown fully to womanhood by now, but it was not the case at all, and the single coupling had left him miserable and distraught for days. His dreams were dashed; this was not how it was supposed to be. She had been his ideal woman for so long, now he found out she was still a girl. The worst thing of all was the knowledge that she was to be the mother of his child. His child! Not some snotty brat that didn't know its manners or how to comport oneself properly.

What would the boy grow up to be like when he had such a wild mother teaching him who knew what kind of terrible things? No, it would not do at all, not at all. So he simply changed his mind, altered his plans and took the burden on himself for the mistakes made, vowing to rectify them. It was for the best really anyway — he should have known it would turn out like this. After all, weren't all women way too much trouble to deal with? Sure, he had minimal experience, mostly consisting of his domineering mother, with intimate encounters limited to a few girls he'd taken pleasure from over the years, but that had never left him feeling much afterward apart from disgust for the giving of themselves so freely to a man they hardly knew.

He had believed Arcene to be different. He had enjoyed her willfulness, loved watching her as she grew older, thinking the independence something to admire, worthy of his children so his offspring too would have such a streak of confidence, be headstrong and know their own minds — it would stand the boys in good stead for what was to come.

Then the reality hit — he couldn't live with a woman like that, couldn't allow such crazy behavior in his household, and he certainly would not stand for such juvenile antics from one that should know better.

He did his best though, kept his intrusions on her mind to a minimum as the baby grew, allowing her to live in comfort and even to share her quarters with her friend Letje — a woman definitely kept under tight control as if not he knew that she would get the upper hand over him sooner or later.

One thing Artek definitely couldn't stand was the gloating of his mother after he had unburdened himself to her, admitting the mistake he had made.

~~~

"I told you she was no good," said Malessa, actually smiling, something she never, ever did.

"You do not have to look so pleased about it Mother, it is most unbecoming. Should you not be showing concern for your son, who has realized he has lost what he believed to be the love of his life, only to find it replaced with a headstrong child that is as wild as the animals themselves?"

"She can't be tamed, she lived too long out there." Malessa pointed out of the window as if all it contained was dirt and shame. "She's feral, like a cat that you expect to sit on your lap when really all it wants to do is rip the heads off things and gouge out your eyes."

"I wouldn't put it quite like that; she is just not to be controlled. She could never be Queen, she'd start eating her food with her hands when we had company, or make my son do unspeakable things like play in the mud and think he was the same as everyone else. Why can't you offer me a shoulder to cry on Mother?"

"Because you deserve your sorrow, you idiot child." Malessa slapped Artek hard across his left cheek.

Artek was so shocked he didn't even raise a hand to his face as was the automatic reaction. "You go too far Mother, much further than I will permit. It was you who wanted me to take a wife, who was to know that Arcene was so uncontrollable?"

"I told you. I told you she was nothing but a savage. It's your fault." Malessa swung out again at Artek's cheek, but he caught the hand and forced it back down.

"Once, you get to do it once. If you so much as dare to mention her name ever again, or raise a hand to me like I am one of your servants, then our time together has come to an end. Do you understand me?"

"How dare you! I am your mother. I gave birth to you; I brought you up in the correct manner. Everything I have done has been for you, and this is how you treat me? Shame on you child."

"Child!? CHILD! I am over a hundred and fifty years old, can control the minds of all, take what I want and do as I wish. I will not be talked to like an imbecile any longer." Artek stamped his foot, the noise from the well polished boot echoing around his opulent quarters before being sucked up by the wall hangings.

"Well act like a man then, rather than a little boy. I didn't bring you up like this. Oh, boo-hoo, poor little Artek, his little child wife turns out to not be what he wanted. So sad, so pitiful. Arcene is useless and so are you. You're no man, you are as much a child as Arcene is, and—"

"I told you never to mention her name again Mother, you had your chance and now it is over."

~~~

Artek stepped over the prone figure of his mother, thick blood oozing out of her throat where he had stabbed deep into her flesh, as cold in life as it would soon be in death. She stared at him with almost lifeless eyes, eyes that didn't believe what had happened.

Artek had no clue how he would feel about the passing of his mother but the one thing he would never have expected was the sudden lightness of spirit he felt, a loosening of his muscles, knots that he never knew he had unraveling in an instant.

He felt buoyant, like he was reborn.

Free.

"If I'd known it could be this simple Mother, I would have done this years ago." Artek frowned as he noticed a spot of blood on his shirt. "See what you've done? Now I shall have to go and get changed."

He turned away from the corpse of his mother and slowly began to unbutton his shirt.

Missing Home

Stanley was as happy as he could possibly be, standing at his favorite spot, at his very own well-stocked pond, fishing rod in hand, the sun shining. What could be better than this? He had food, he had water, he had his house to repair and he had the beautiful, if overgrown gardens to wander around and slowly get to grips with.

Life was perfect.

Finally he had found his sense of place, his position in the world as one of caretaker for a property that had once been grand and would be again. There was much to do, yet he felt no guilt for his leisure activity. There was no rush, after all he had all the time in the world.

Some things could wait; fishing could not.

Stanley felt himself begin to get sleepy, the sun was lulling him into an almost hypnotic trance, so he reeled in the line and moved back into the shade of the large willow.

He really was the luckiest man alive.

~~~

Stanley woke up to absolute quiet. No birds were singing, no insects were chirping, he couldn't even hear the sound of the frogs in the pond — something that was usually a constant at this time of the year.

He opened his eyes, confused by the presence of a ceiling. What was happening? Where was he?

A dream, he had just been having a dream. He was in his cell, the same room he'd been in for years now.

The only time he was ever happy was when he managed to sleep and not have nightmares.

A Long Day

"Make it stop Letje, make it stop. I don't like it, I don't like it at all. Argh. Ow ow ow. Aaaaaaargh. What was that? What's going on? Is it over? Is it done? Letje? Pleeeeeeease."

Letje tried to get some feeling back into her hand but it was no use, Arcene was gripping so tightly she didn't have a chance of being able to free herself. All she could do was try to calm her down, which wasn't easy. It had been going on for hours now and there was no end in sight yet. "It's okay, I'm here, I'm here. Hush, try to take deep breaths like we practiced. Remember?"

Arcene was soaked in sweat, her hair plastered to the side of her face, forehead shining and her normally pale skin was bright red. Her face was puffy and somewhat blotchy and as she tried to breathe in a controlled fashion she interrupted herself again to scream.

"Letje, make it stop. Ugh, ugh, ugh... Argh. I'm being ripped open. It's torture. What's happening? Why is this happening to me? I didn't do anything wrong, why am I being tortured?"

"Hush now, it's alright, don't worry, you're just having a baby is all - perfectly natural."

"But something's wrong, this can't be normal... Argh. Why me? I'm a good girl. Aaaaarggh."

Letje smiled. "Well, I wouldn't go that far. Just calm down, nothing's wrong, this is what happens when you have a baby, everything's fine. You've got hours yet, this is just the beginning, you just started labor, you aren't even that dilated yet."

"Dilated? What isn't very dilated? And... ugh, ugh, ugh, no way is this normal. Nobody would have babies if it was as bad as this. Hew hew hew, hew hew hew."

"That's it, good girl, keep doing your breathing, you'll get there, you will be fine. Just relax." Letje didn't have the heart to tell her that it seemed like she was actually having a very easy labor so far but that it would get a lot worse very soon. Arcene was only young but many fifteen year olds had children as there was always the risk of Lethargy rearing its ugly head. It became commonplace for those as young as thirteen to bear children, something that used to be the norm even in the UK since many years before The Lethargy.

In some regards post Lethargy UK was a lot like Victorian Britain in terms of how such things were thought of. Letje wasn't concerned about how the labor had gone so far, she was more concerned with how it was going to go when the time came to give birth. Arcene was a slim child, woman, she must think of her as a woman now, she would be a mother very soon, and Letje's main concern was that the birth would go smoothly. Arcene had stayed very slender right through her pregnancy and her hips were still as narrow and tomboyish as they had ever been - it wasn't a good sign at all.

Letje had read up all that she could, learning about how the hips widened as pregnancies progressed, or did so in most cases, but Arcene seemed hardly changed at all in physical appearance apart from the bump of her baby where the skin was so taut Arcene had voiced her concerns countless times that her skin would just split and the baby would pop out onto the floor while she tried to stop the rest of her insides from spilling out after him.

To put it mildly, Arcene had been, and still was, not wholly in-tune with either her pregnancy or becoming a mother.

Letje didn't blame her in the slightest.

It's all that damn—

"Letje! What was that? What's happening? Is he out? Have I had a baby? Phew phew phew... Argh."

"No, afraid not, just a bit longer to go yet. Stay calm, it's not good for you to get so worked up." Letje shook her hand gratefully as Arcene released her iron grip. Her hand was as white as Arcene's hair but it slowly turned red as the blood rushed to fill the cut off veins and arteries.

"Hey! What are you doing? You can't move, you're having a baby. Lie back down."

Arcene had her legs over the side of the bed, her favorite kilt a mess of blood and amniotic fluid from when her waters had broken a few hours ago — a sure sign things were not as they should be. "I'm not staying in that bed any longer, and I am not having this baby. It hurts too much, I don't want to do it. I'm going for a walk, and I want to see Leel, and Gamm. Where are they? Why aren't they here?"

"You know why, you shouldn't ask. And be careful, you aren't in any condition to be walking, you're having a baby Arcene, you need to lie down."

"Well I don't want to and I want to see them and I want to go home to The Commorancy and I want to see Marcus and Fasolt, even if he has got the stupidest bony bum. Argh."

"Arcene!" Letje rushed over to Arcene and grabbed her just before she crumpled to the floor — she had let go of the side of the bed and was half way across the room before she began to fall. Letje was there in an instant, Awoken reflexes firing off neurons at double her pre-Awoken speed. Letje put her arms under Arcene from behind, grasped one in the other and pulled her up.

"I feel horrible. Look at my belly, my skins going to rip and look at all those red stretch marks on my tummy. It used to be all flat. I could see my muscles now I'm all fat and ruined and it hurts and I want something to eat."

Aha, that will work, thought Letje, brightening as a distraction came instantly to mind.

"Mm, I'm hungry too. I wonder what would be the best to have right about now? I kind of fancy a nice big slab of beef with mustard and fresh bread, or maybe with potatoes and gravy, and a nice cup of tea too. What about you?"

Arcene visibly brightened. Some things never changed and food was, and always had been, a total obsession for the young mother-to-be. She didn't even notice Letje helping her back to the bed while she voiced her thoughts on what she would like to eat.

"Do we have beef? That would be lovely. Ooh, or what about chicken? The way you do it when you fry it and make it all crispy on the outside and inside it's lovely and white and we always burn our hands as we can't wait to eat it. Agh, urgh."

"We? You mean you, as you always try to eat it too fast, you always have done. Remember when we first met and you stole my rabbit, you were the same back then."

"Hehe, I re— ow, argh, uh oh. Wassat? What happened? Argh. Letje, help please I think I'm breaking again. Argh."

"Okay okay, hang on, lay back, I'm just going to take a look and see how things are doing. Stay calm, think about chicken and potatoes."

"Argh, hurry up Letje, it's not working, I can't think of food, something must be wrong, something must be really wrong."

Letje went cold. It didn't look right, even in her limited experience. Her non-existent experience. She had read books, watched the supplied recordings closely and over and over again, but nothing had prepared her for quite how messy and scary it all was, and Arcene hadn't even given birth yet.

Beep beep beep beep beeeeeeeeeeeeeeeep. Beep beep beep beep beeeeeeeeeeeep.

"What's that? What's happening?"

"Don't worry, just the stupid monitor, I think it's faulty." Letje turned it down as there was little to be gained from Arcene getting even more stressed out. But it wasn't going according to plan, not that this had been the plan at all anyway. "Okay, here we go. Are you ready?"

Arcene wriggled so was more upright in bed and looked at Letje with pure and utter fear. "Ready for what?" she asked cautiously, like events had sneaked up on her.

"Ready to have a baby silly. Are you ready?"

Arcene flopped back onto the pillows heavily. "No, I don't want to."

"Well, tough. Get ready to push."

"Push what?"

"Push the baby out. You're going to feel it any minute now and then I want you to squeeze down like we practiced and push as hard as you can, okay?"

"Argh. Nooooooooooooooooooooo. Phew phew phew, grrrrrrrrrrrrrrrr."

"Good, again."

"Phew phew phew, grrrrrrrrrrrrrrrrrr."

"Here it comes, her it comes. Push."

"Grrrrrrrrrrrrrrrrrrrrrrrrrr. Ugh, help Letje, it hurts it hurts so much, stop it stop it now."

"Just a little longer but take some breaths, relax."

"RELAX?!"

"Okay, try to relax then, just think calm thoughts. The baby has moved down, I think it won't be long now."

It went on for hours.

~~~

Arcene was drenched. Not just damp with sweat but soaked from head to toe and shining like she'd just emerged from the ocean; she smelled just as salty. She also smelled like old seaweed rotting on the shoreline. It had gone on all through the afternoon and into the night, now the moon watched the scene through the window, shining pale lunar light on the struggle to continue the human race.

It hadn't gone well and it wasn't over yet.

Letje reached out for Arcene's hand and her grip slipped as Arcene's palms were so slick. The poor thing lay back against the sodden pillows completely exhausted as tears trickled slowly down her burning cheeks. Arcene's labor was as complicated as she herself was. No sooner did Letje think that the contractions were getting short and it was time for her to give birth, than they receded somewhat and the whole process was repeated over again.

Letje wiped her wet hand on her overall and went to check again.

"This time. This time Arcene, we have to do it now or you will be too tired," said Letje excitedly.

"Hmm?" mumbled Arcene, so exhausted she didn't seem to care any longer. "Argh. What's happening?"

"It's coming, for real this time. Okay, let's do the exercises. You ready?"

"Ugh, argh. Nope, but okay."

"Pant, pant, push"! shouted Letje.

"Phew, phew, argh."

"Good. Again."

"Phew, phew, aaaaaaaaaaaaaargh."

"Good. Okay, I can see the top of his head, not long now."

"You can? Cool. Aaaaaaaaaaaaaaaaaaaargh. I'm being ripped, stop it Letje. Argh."

Arcene dilated as the baby crowned, her perineum stretching tight and paper thin, a tear beginning. "Hang in there, here he comes. Push. Push harder. Harder. One more."

"Argh, ugh, grrrrrrrrrrr. Grrrrrrrr, ugh."

Waaaaaaaaaaaaaaaaaaaaaaaaaaaaaaa. Waaaaaaaaaaaa. Waaaaaaaaaaaaaaaa.

"That's it, you did it. It is a boy; he's lovely." Letje placed the wailing baby on to Arcene's chest where it instantly clenched its tiny fingers around her finger and promptly fell asleep.

"He looks weird, is he alright?"

Letje smiled. "He's fine, he's just a little goopy and needs a clean up. He's perfect."

"I can't believe I did it. Thank you Letje. Hello little man, and how are you? You took a while you know? Mummy and Letje have been having a hard time of—"

"Thank you, I'll be taking that." Artek snatched the newborn from Arcene's chest while Letje stood there doing nothing as it happened.

The door closed behind them.

There was a shift in the atmosphere, as if time had been reversed a few seconds, which to all intents and purposes it had.

"Is it over? Have I had him?" said Arcene, coming back to herself now that Artek was gone. "Ugh, I feel something."

"Huh? Oh, what?"

No, not this time, this is enough. Letje knew she had been violated, she was beginning to remember already.

No more lost memories, she remembered them all. It came flooding back to her in vivid detail, month after month of forced forgetfulness, coming to and not understanding how Arcene was so pregnant and now the baby was gone, ripped from its mother seconds after its birth.

"Letje? I feel funny. Am I having the baby?"

"No Arcene, it's the placenta. You already had the baby."

Arcene sobbed into her pillow as she passed the afterbirth of her missing baby boy.

This Could be a Problem

Arcene was utterly exhausted. She was on the verge of death, that much was obvious. The birth had been long and dangerous, the hours leading up to it fraught with complications, and Letje was sure that neither her or the child was going to survive. All the while their lives were lived in a haze of half-memories, falsehoods and forgetfulness.

Arcene simply wasn't suited to bringing life into the world, not yet. Her body was still that of a child — years of living from one desperate meal to the next meant that she had not developed as quickly as many of her age, if they were lucky enough to have slightly more regular feeding and didn't have to be quite as self-reliant. The result was a very slim body, tall and becoming quite lanky, but still rather flat-chested and narrow at the hip. When Letje had looked deep enough into the body of what she still thought of as a child, even though Arcene was fifteen, she could see that her friend hadn't accepted the pregnancy as well as she might have: hormones were not quite right, her body hadn't quite got ready for caring for the child that had just been born. Milk ducts hadn't adapted correctly so it would be a struggle to rear a baby by breastfeeding.

Letje could see that Arcene's pelvic girdle was stretched to snapping, and the prolonged delivery had drained her of every ounce of energy, coming close to eating up the last of her life force, sending her to The Void before she got the chance to finally deliver the child that seemed to know that it was safer inside its mother than outside in the world where it was ripped away from her, Arcene believing she'd never seen him or even had the chance to nestle on her chest and greet the reluctant mother before she slept the sleep of the dead. Letje would help her to remember, she had to at least have that brief memory of her baby clutching at her — it was too precious to let Artek take that away too.

It was now twenty four hours later and as Letje walked into the room, the air thick with the lingering odors of birth and what came afterward, she came to a halt like she'd slammed into the invisible walls of The Shower Room.

What has she done? What has she done? Oh my god, I can't believe it. You stupid girl.

Arcene was still sat in bed, sweaty even though Letje had cajoled, then finally forced, her into the shower after she'd slept for what must have been eight hours after giving birth. Yet now she was slick with a sheen of sweat like she was still in the throes of labor. Her silver hair was plastered to the side of her head, sticking to her shoulders, unkempt, knotted and crazy.

Worst were Arcene's eyes: they were dark hollows, the life almost gone from them. Unfocused, unsteady and uncaring.

Like she's just stopped thinking. I can't blame her for that.

Arcene was slumped into the pile of pillows like a dead weight. She just lay there, unseeing, body still beneath the thin sheet that covered her nakedness. Leel sat to the side, head resting on the bed; Arcene wasn't even stroking her head.

Things are worse than I thought.

But even Arcene's inattentiveness to her beloved new pet was as nothing compared to what Letje could see beneath the surface of her young friend. Arcene had Awoken. Letje saw the signs not long after the birth, saw the changes happening within Arcene that signaled the beginning of a true Awakening, not a partial one. A true Awakening that would see her grow in power as she aged and understood the gifts she now had, to become much more than merely Whole — the Awakening that Arcene had been saying she wanted for years now, forever whining it wasn't fair that Letje was Awoken and she wasn't.

Letje had felt her too young, certainly still too immature, although she had grown up considerably over recent years, but now it seemed that the decision had been taken out of her hands — Arcene was truly Awoken, had power from The Noise, and had the ability to alter her own body chemistry at will. She had done a terrible thing with her abilities.

"What have you done? Arcene, you can't change it back you know? You're stuck now. Forever." Letje wanted to simultaneously shout and scream, hit and kick at the prone figure, grab her, hold her tight, and cry for the static future that Arcene had inflicted on herself. Letje wept for the things her friend had done, for the girl she thought of as a daughter, forever a child in her eyes, now no longer just the feelings of her older companion, but a reality she had inflicted on herself for the rest of her life.

"Go away. Leave me alone," said Arcene moodily from the bed. "I don't want to talk to you. I don't want to talk to anybody. Ever."

"But why? Why have you done this?"

Arcene opened he eyes angrily and stared into the very soul of Letje. "Why?" she shouted, spittle hitting her chin, Leel whimpering and trotting over to Letje where she patted her head to tell her everything would be alright, even though it wouldn't. "Why? So that I stay like this. So that no other man will try to do what Artek did. He's a pervert, sleeping with young girls before their time, but I won't let anyone else do it to me, not ever. I'm just a girl," she sobbed, tears soaking into the pillows. "I didn't like it Letje. I don't want to have babies and have them taken from me, so I've stopped all that, and I will not grow any older than I am now. I'm staying like this and there's nothing you can do about it."

It was true, there was nothing Letje could do for her dearest friend. It had been Arcene's decision, albeit one she was in no fit state to make, and the result was irreparable. Arcene had stopped her body clock, she would never, ever, for as long as she lived, age another day. Letje could see it, understood that Arcene had that power within her, something very few Awoken could control with such depth of certainty.

That wasn't all, she would no longer ovulate, hormones had been altered so that Arcene could never again conceive a child, she was to stay as a pre-pubescent now and for always. She'd had her moment of puberty and now it was reversed — she was back to how her body performed a few years previously, when she truly was still a child. Arcene looked her age but she would never grow to look a day older even if she lived to be a thousands years, which was a very distinct possibility.

Unless she does anything else stupid.

Letje went to her, to her friend, the broken wreck of a woman now a child again, and hugged her tight. What else could she do? She cuddled her, stroked out the limp hair, and whispered nonsense in her ear while they cried — both of them weeping for the things that had been done to Arcene, the world they lived in and what had been lost. More than anything though, they cried for the baby — the baby that was to be Arcene's only chance at motherhood, ripped from her arms by a man they both hated more than anything else in the world.

Nothing but emptiness remained. Emptiness and tears.

The rest of the world was as nothing in comparison to the loss of innocence, something that could never be returned once stolen, however much they both wanted it.

Arcene was a girl, a woman for a brief moment but now she would always be what lay crumpled in the bed, weeping for countless sorrows, waking to the reality of what she had done and what had been taken away from her.

"I want my baby. Where's my baby Letje?" sobbed Arcene, stroking Leel who sat obediently by the bed once more.

"I don't know Arcene, but we'll find him. I promise."

"And we'll kill Artek, won't we?"

"You can count on that. If it's the last thing we do then he will die for what he's done to you, for what he's done to countless others. He'll pay alright — with blood."

"Good."

"Do you remember? We've been tricked Arcene, in a daze, our memories taken from us. But do you remember your baby?"

Please let her remember. At least give her something.

Arcene stared at her through drooping eyelids. "I remember," she said, smiling for the first time in days." Then her face darkened. "I remember it all now Letje, everything that has happened."

"Me too, me too."

Arcene was asleep, her body depleted almost to extinction. Letje knew that she was lucky to be alive, the labor and birth had almost killed her, and what she had done to herself in her state of sorrow could well have been the end for her, but somehow she'd pulled up hidden reserves, changed herself forever, and managed to survive with the consequences of her rash actions.

Letje would let her sleep. She had things to do, important things if they were ever to finish what had turned into the worst of times.

Letje walked to the door, turned when she heard a whimper, but it was just Leel jumping up on the bed, cuddling in tight to her mistress. Letje left her there. At least when she woke up Arcene would have a familiar face to greet her — unconditional love, she certainly needed it.

Letje wandered down the echoing hall, knowing that what she was going to uncover was going to see the nightmare they found themselves in continue for a long time to come.

Maybe it would never end.

Baby Theft

It was a shame, so much time invested in the girl. He had thought she was so sweet but she turned out to be entirely unsuitable for one such as him. Artek hated to admit it but his mother had been right. Oh how she would be smiling if only she could see him now, but it was he that was smiling — she was in The Void, where she belonged.

Waaaaaaaaaaaaaaaaaaaa.

Artek peered down at the newborn child, his son and heir, and tickled him gently under the chin. He clutched the boy tight, vowing that he would never treat his own child as his mother had treated him. Sure, there would be rules, what was life without rules? But the coldness? The aloofness and lack of love? No, he would never treat any child of his in such a manner.

Artek spoke to Ahebban through The Noise, telling him to speed up, to head to the east and he had better be quick about it if he knew what was good for him.

Behind them was a long convoy of horses from various herds, only the strongest and largest, the rest slaughtered, butchered by captive men who were dispatched quickly once their work was done. Now the dried meat was carried by oblivious parents or offspring, fortunate in one way only: they didn't know what their loads contained. Ahebban knew though, and he knew that as the days, weeks and months passed then the convoy would dwindle as more meat was consumed.

The people were entirely minimal in the convoy however — Artek had decided that hardly any of the countless thousands of people he had kept alive until very recently would be worthy subjects, so an epic cleansing had taken place in the days leading up to his child's birth until all that now remained were those he felt absolutely essential to the future of his rule. They were mostly adults, but also a few children that he saw potential in and believed would be suitable playmates for the heir apparent, although his son would remain prince for many centuries to come.

And the wet nurse of course. He couldn't very well have a child without a female to breastfeed his son. The woman's own child was born with The Lethargy and was promptly dispatched — no point wasting valuable milk and emotion on a child that would die anyway.

Artek congratulated himself on his practical thinking, although even he had squirmed at such a decision and the end to the child's life was done by another, a man that was himself put to death soon after, this time by Artek's own hand.

As those left alive at Bridewell slowly came to their senses, realizing what had happened to them, so Artek and his small retinue were already miles away. He found it strange to be out in the open with his new child, and it certainly wasn't what he had expected from his future. But if truth be told he was actually rather surprised at how good he felt — the freedom was exhilarating. This hadn't been the plan, he'd expected to marry Arcene, get annoyed by his mother for eternity, and rule a country that comprised Whole people that were suitable as his subjects. Now everything was turned upside down. He'd pretty much eliminated everyone apart from a few, and that would mean his plans were seriously compromised, but in a way he understood it had all worked out for the best.

Now he had time. Time to bring up a son, time to find a properly suitable Queen for himself and a wife for his own child when he was old enough, and with the country devoid of human life for the most part he could pick and choose where to go — there were still pockets of life he hadn't had the time to look into yet, so the chances were good that somewhere, sometime, he would find what he was looking for.

In the meantime he was happy just to be out from under the clutches of his mother, glad that he'd seen the light when it came to Arcene, yet after all that he had changed his mind he'd still felt enough for her to allow her to keep her life, and for Letje to be left alive too. He'd thought long and hard about that, finally deciding that she would be of more use alive than dead. After all, she was needed to run The Commorancy, there were still people there behind its mysterious walls and they needed her to allow them to Awaken — he could deal with her in the future, and it was always fun to see just who came out of The Commorancy and what they had to offer once they were truly Awoken to their full potential.

Artek headed east, day after day, running Ahebban and the other horses hard, heading for a future he knew was going to be just perfect. After all, who was there to stop him from making it exactly what he wanted it to be?

~~~

Gamm was bound with his hands behind his back, a long length of rope securing him to one of the horses in the middle of the convoy, just as a few others were. The small group of people were mostly sat upon the horses but Gamm was deemed too large and heavy to do anything but walk. After all, Artek had to ensure the horses made it in good health for as long as they were required.

Lost in a haze of forgetfulness, Gamm found it impossible to recall much of anything. He knew his name, remembered some of his past, even half-formed memories of staying in The Commorancy, and he recalled quite vividly being given his Ink, as much a part of him now as anything else. He had a picture in his mind of a strange bulbous head, sharp teeth and a strange hissing voice, but he didn't connect it to his Ink.

He trudged along, awareness clouded, until one day his Ink began to glow ever so slightly. He paid it no mind, unsure whether or not it had always done such a thing — uncaring either way, lost in a dream where all there was to do was walk, eat, sleep and feel content with his lot, unknowing of what he once was, what he could possibly be again.

Empty Halls, Empty Promises

I promised her everything would be alright. And it isn't.

It was far from alright, and Letje almost, but not quite, let the misery overwhelm her. There was one saving grace: Bird had come. He nuzzled her ear with his dangerous beak, then took flight, gliding down the empty corridors that made up the prison, or Bridewell, as it was perversely known. Death camp would have been more appropriate. Letje poked a finger into the deep hole Bird had made as he had landed, the blood dull in the low light, power sources turned off, no longer needed by Artek — he'd left.

Letje had already walked some of the halls, narrow corridors and open spaces of the place that had held almost all the remaining Whole of the United Kingdom prisoner at some point or other. She'd known it was deserted the minute she came out of her dream-state a few hours after Arcene's baby was taken. There were puzzles upon puzzles that haunted her, and she understood that she had to get to the root of exactly what had happened — she knew she wasn't going to like what she found.

Artek had left, that much was clear. He'd left and his spell had been lifted. Too much had been done to too many people for the effects to last after he no longer cared whether they recalled their imprisonment. He had what he wanted, or at least a part of what he wanted anyway.

So much came flooding back to Letje in a barrage of memories it was hard not to collapse under the weight of it all. The things the man had done, the things he'd dome to so many people, but especially to Arcene. How could she have let it happen?

Because I didn't remember, that's why. I tried to stop him countless times and each time he simply made me forget. Like ripping pages out of a book and rewriting the story. Time, after time, after time.

It had been elven months since they had first stood outside the gates and had a brief conversation with Artek and his mother — some kind of convoluted plan half-formed in Letje's mind about letting them be captured so she could infiltrate them, discover what exactly they had been doing and if anyone they had taken was still alive. Letje had thought herself powerful, she was, after all, more adept in The Noise than almost anybody else, and had better control over her body than she had thought possible.

But it wasn't enough. If you dedicate yourself to one aspect of what is obtainable once Awoken then you can surpass all others, and Artek Ligertwood had clearly spent his entire very extended life perfecting techniques so that he could get his own way at all times — he was the master of memory manipulation. You could live the same few seconds over and over for a lifetime and you would never know it unless he decided he was bored and let you come back to your own reality intact — most never had that luxury, they were killed in the middle of their dream lives, never knowing if it was the first time they had tried to cross him, or the millionth. Either way, it ended up being the last for the majority.

Letje continued her exploring, knowing that Arcene was sleeping, that what she had done had almost taken everything away from her. No matter what she looked like there was now no escaping the fact that Arcene was a grown woman — such acts committed against her had forever taken away her innocence. Letje just hoped that not all of it was gone for good.

Letje was a failure, she'd let everyone down and now they were either dead or gone. How could she not have seen it? She was strong, powerful and deadly, yet Artek had got the better of her so easily. It was unforgivable and Letje still didn't understand how he could exert such influence, yet knowing at the same time that such things were possible, and much more besides.

It would be avenged; Arcene would have her son back.

~~~

Letje sat in the small cell, staring at the body of Umeko, beautiful even in death. She had hunted but there was no sign of the others, not alive anyway. Stanley, poor dear Stanley, he was gone. She found him in his cell, just like Umeko, like he'd just been turned off as Artek had decided he wasn't worth the trouble. Kirstie was nowhere to be found, so at least there was a little hope, and she dare not think what had become of Umeko's family. She just prayed they were alive, being kept safe by Artek as he felt them worthy of his rule.

Umeko lay on the thin mattress on the cot, serene and still, never to put on her makeup again, never to draw others to her with her beauty both inner and outer.

Letje left her, going from cell to cell, level to level, checking through the building thoroughly — there was nobody left alive, just her and Arcene, nothing else but death and the remnants of Artek's corruption.

It was time to go; there was nothing left here. They wouldn't find peace within these walls, nobody ever had, now nobody ever would.

All that was left was what was outside.

Letje went to check the extensive grounds — just in case.

A Habit's a Habit

Mother Superior understood it was time to move, the only problem was that the decomposing bodies of her Sisters were rather a hindrance. They were piled on top of her, making it impossible to move more than her head, and even that hurt her neck. She hissed curse after curse through razor sharp teeth, calling forth all manner of demonic forces that had become part of her religion as it warped and grew over the centuries to accommodate the world she found herself and her many generations of Sisters living in, only her watching them all unfold, the others never Awakening, just living Whole lives, each and every one of them. In the entire history of The Sisters Of The Lethargy this was the first time a single Sister had died by anything but natural causes — Mother Superior would have her revenge and it would be terrible.

That foul man with his red hair and his green shirts and his impossibly smug smile, how she hated him with a vengeance she never knew she possessed.

He would die and it would be the most terrible of deaths, she would see to it if it was her last act on earth before she made her way to The Void to join her Sisters.

She was actually surprised that she had managed to survive, and not a lot surprised Mother Superior, mostly as she couldn't care less about anything apart from her Sisters and a continuation of her religious order. When that sadistic man Victor had first begun entering the cells and dispatching the men that had served The Sisters for so long she had been annoyed and angry that such valuable resources were being wasted, but when he began beating on The Sisters, then unceremoniously slitting their throats, well, she was livid.

It went on for hours, him entering the cells, the screams rising as beating after beating was administered, until Victor realized that he was getting tired from all the dragging of corpses and made the remaining Sisters and their men walk out into the space designated for quadrant 5 so he could save himself the trouble of carrying them. Then the horrors mounted as he made The Sisters watch while he walked down the line they were standing in and picked one at random, beating her terribly in front of the others before cutting her throat and throwing the small body onto the growing pile.

The Sisters didn't scream anymore, didn't show fear or try to run: they knew there was nowhere to go. If this was to be the way they entered The Void then they would do so with dignity; Mother Superior was immensely proud of the way they greeted The End.

Then it was her turn. She was pulled forward roughly, waving goodbye to the remaining Sisters before she blacked out as a huge hand slammed into the side of her head. She was conscious again in a second and this time she was ready — she let herself slip between the cracks of reality, went deep into The Noise and settled there to wait. She watched with interest as the small body she had inhabited for centuries was pummeled mercilessly, then as it crumpled to the ground Victor bent and with his dark-stained knife he swiped it across her throat, the cut going deep, blood pouring out.

Her body was thrown onto the pile and soon more bodies were added. Mother Superior could feel the weight of her Sisters but much heavier was the weight of her responsibility as the life force ebbed out of her.

She was almost gone, but not quite. Mother Superior focused deeply and as she did so her Ink shone as bright as the clearest of skies. Energy flowed through her decorated skin, a clear energy that was The Noise in concentrated form, the power given by all the Sisters combined, immensely potent in one such as her — truly Awoken. She sent it to where it was needed, focusing the energy on the slash across her throat where her decorative tattoos were sliced in two. Energy that was almost as clear as water and had substance jumped from one split end of The Ink to the other, connecting the pieces, reaching deeper and deeper, fixing the damage to the skin, penetrating flesh, sealing the wound, repairing it so the energy could flow freely once more.

Mother Superior departed The Noise as the work neared completion, and she watching internally as her body slowly produced more blood to compensate for what was lost.

She felt the burden of her Sisters once more, and there was a promise made: those responsible would die. She would remain on the earth until justice was done; her Sisters would not go without their recompense for the crimes committed.

It took a long time for the repairs to be complete, then Mother Superior put her body into stasis, awareness all but lost, biding her time, waiting for an opportunity, a sign that she would be able to escape and have her revenge.

Months passed, empty days and nights where she hibernated, knowing nothing, just waiting. Her time would come.

She slowly began to surface from her dreams, then days later, sensing the difference in the air, the knowledge that those she sought had either died or left, she opened her eyes for the first time since her ordeal began and stared at the horrors so close to her face. Her beautiful Sisters, so pure and dedicated, nothing more than stinking rags and covered in flies.

She would avenge them, nothing would stand in her way.

First she just had to find a way to get out from under the pile of their corpses.

~~~

Letje unlocked the thick door made up of steel bars and walked out into the large courtyard for quadrant 5 and promptly nearly turned right back around when she saw the piles of bodies. Mound after mound of them, large and small, smoldering or bloody, every act that resulted in the death of a person carried out, clearly some of the deaths committed over extended periods of time, and with delight.

Something caught her eye though, a hint of red and green in the far corner, close to the fence, before the death scene was repeated in the next enclosure, and on and on it went, seemingly into infinity.

Letje walked through a cloud of flies, shutting down olfactory senses to suppress the gag reflex, and picked her way between fresh or rotting corpses, heading towards the body she recognized. It was her, Artek's mother, no paler in death than she had been in life, although she was somewhat greener. It was strange, as Letje could tell just looking at her that the body had been cold for a long time, many months, yet there was no rot, no maggots eating her eyes, no sign that this wasn't a body freshly killed. But it wasn't the case, Melissa had entered The Void many months ago, her life force and energy accumulated from The Noise over centuries slowly seeping out over almost the whole term of Arcene's pregnancy — the power so strong it would take many more months to dissipate.

It was a strange sight, and Letje couldn't help wondering if maybe a part of Melissa was still in there somewhere, aware of the energy slowly fading, no final rest for the likes of her, a ghost that was trapped in the body, just waiting for it all to be forgotten — like a victim of The Lethargy that just slowly faded away, a little death happening every day until finally there came peace.

"Over here. I'm trapped," came a voice from behind, barely more than a whisper. More a hiss than a normal human voice.

Letje felt like a fool. As soon as she heard it The Noise lit up the small but very powerful presence like a bonfire — now was not the time to be lax and let surprises that were easy to look for creep up on her. Letje knew she had to stay constantly vigilant, and was annoyed with herself for such a basic lack of care — her life, Arcene's, her baby's and countless other lives depending on her now. She had not done well so far so she should know better.

The hiss of a voice came again, directing Letje even though she could clearly sense the presence of life. As she walked toward the survivor Letje shut down the effects of the devastating carnage that surrounded her.

The number of bodies was breathtaking, there must have been thousands. No doubt there would be more, many more, some still inside the building in the few places she had yet to search, others buried in the fields outside the fences — there was no mistaking the large rectangular patches of bare earth, meters to a side, that were the mass graves of those found unsuitable for life by Artek and his mother before she too was seen as surplus to requirements.

Nuns, it's small nuns. The ones that guided us here.

Letje wept silently for the scale of the atrocities, not understanding what Artek hoped to achieve by such actions, but nonetheless it was done, and she had failed to do what she had set out to do: stop him from destroying what was left of the population. How could she have been so easily outmaneuvered? It was shameful. But it wasn't too late, she would finish what she had begun.

Carefully, and with the utmost respect, Letje cradled the small bodies on the pile, bulbous heads lolling like the dolls she had never owned from centuries past, and one by one she lifted them from the pile before placing them on the ground. Mother Superior watched her silently and Letje didn't say a thing; there was nothing to be said, just a job to be done. Letje got the feeling Mother Superior was a woman that talked little anyway, and when actions spoke louder than words there was no need to fill the silence. She was beyond such banalities, and Letje was glad of it.

Eventually the bodies were removed and Mother Superior was free. Her habit was in tatters, ripped from her beating, and the washed-out gray was hard to discern beneath so much dried blood. Letje held out a hand for the strange small woman, who took it without hesitation. It was a child's hand, yet wrinkled and dry, but there was great power there, and Letje spotted Ink running from her fingertips up her arm, hidden by her habit. The large head was bare, gray hair visible, and dancing underneath, covering the entire dome of her head, tracing down the back of her neck, curving around ears before disappearing, were incredibly complex patterns, raised and proud, energy flowing through them, pulsing and rushing like a stream after a flood.

Letje didn't think she had met a stranger person in her life, but then she realized the nonsense of such thoughts — had she not just rescued Marcus, a man that was triplicate? And Fasolt, what stranger man was there than that? Or maybe when she crouched by the side of a pool until her legs cramped and conversed through The Noise with a man that was no longer a man but was a sentient hivemind in the form of crayfish? Yes, when she looked at it like that then Mother Superior was rather normal in comparison, just odd looking.

"Thank you," said Mother Superior, voice hissing like a snake, air whistling between her strange teeth, the mouth as thin as the livid scar across her throat.

"You are welcome. I am Letje, and I assume you are Mother Superior?"

"I am. We have justice to deliver I believe," said Mother Superior, staring at her Sisters, her face creasing in distaste.

"We do indeed. It's just a matter of finding him first. He's gone, and he took my friend's baby with him. His baby too, but he stole him from Arcene."

Mother Superior waved away such nonsense. She cared nothing for Letje, her friend, the baby or anything apart from revenge for the death of her own kind.

She's a strange one, and no mistake.

"We will find Artek, that foul man. We will kill the man that did this to my Sisters," hissed Mother Superior.

"Well, we just need to know where to start," said Letje.

Mother Superior stood motionless, eyes rolling back in her head, before then quickly staring at her arms, spinning slowly in a circle, stopping when the Ink pulsed brighter. "We shall find them. Gamm, he was here with you?" Letje nodded. "And now he is with Artek. We shall follow them." Letje nodded again — it was clear Mother Superior was not going to be big on conversation.

Gone

"What do you mean gone? What do you mean they stole Arcene's baby? What happened?"

"I mean we woke up and there were thousands of bodies all dead, and they had gone and he had taken Arcene's baby with him. At least I hope he did," said Letje, looking worriedly at Arcene. "Sorry."

"He took my baby, and I'm going to get him back. And she's going to help." Arcene pointed to Mother Superior, who had remained silent, still stunned by the small portion of The Commorancy she had seen upon arrival as they made their way to the kitchen.

"I guess I'll have to go and deal with this mess myself then, won't I?" said Marcus, eyes flashing dangerously: black then blue, then darker than Letje's shame.

Letje was a child, a useless little girl that couldn't do anything right. Couldn't save her friend from the sorrow no woman should ever know, and here she was, standing before the most powerful man she had ever met, feeling unworthy, knowing that she had failed and that it might be too late now. After all, it had taken them months to get back to The Commorancy. Arcene was like a person lost to The Lethargy, and the trip was slow and arduous, having to rest for days on end between short bursts of activity.

What a mess.

Now Marcus was going to take over and Letje would never be in charge of The Commorancy again — he wouldn't trust her if she couldn't even take care of the matter she had been sent to deal with.

"Ugh." Letje woke from the dream, shivering and pulling her blanket tighter around her shoulders. She'd been having similar dreams for days now, each time waking and feeling inadequate. Her confidence was knocked, the dreams telling her that she was out of her depth, no match for those that were much older and wiser than herself.

She had to keep reminding herself that this was at the crux of the matter though: Artek was a lot older than her, had been able to hone his skills probably to perfection long before she had even been born. He would have been setting plans into motion even before he Awoke at The Commorancy, which was many normal lifetimes ago. No wonder he had got the better of her; she was silly to have expected to have come out victorious when dealing with such a man.

Letje poked the fire, adding a few thin sticks, then a larger branch on top. The heat rose along with her confidence.

She may still be young and inexperienced but she was powerful. She would become victorious and she would resume her rule of The Commorancy, the job entrusted to her by Marcus, guarantees given that she was to continue to be the caretaker once she returned — with answers.

There was no way she would go home before the matter was settled — this was her task, her responsibility. Her mess. Letje looked over at the sleeping figures of Arcene and Leel, bonded as never before over the recent days, Arcene clinging to her for comfort more often than she sought out Letje's embrace, or Letje went to her when she was obviously finding it hard to continue.

Mother Superior was sat opposite Letje, staring at the fire, a wicked grin on her impish face, large head flickering with the shadows from the fire. She had cleaned her habit best she could, repaired it with patches taken from the clothing of her Sisters, and as far as Letje knew, the woman never slept.

Here was another Awoken that made Letje's life so far seem insignificant. The woman was older than Marcus or even Fasolt, the oldest person she had ever met, and there were depths to her that Letje could only guess at. Conversation with the strange nun was stilted bordering on impossible, and as she showed little interest in talking anyway Letje had spoken just a handful of words to her since she had freed her from the pile of corpses. There had been no gushing thank-yous, no talks about what had happened and the plans for the future, all there was between them was the pulsing of her Ink and the direction she took — Letje, Arcene and Leel followed, there was nothing else to do.

The only consolation to the whole sorry mess, and the terrible destruction of the already limited population, was the glaring fact that not only had Artek managed to easily take Mother Superior and her entire Sisterhood, keeping them under his spell for so long, but he had managed to fool Marcus easily too, something that Letje would have believed impossible. So it wasn't just her that had failed and been enthralled by his skills, it was the oldest and most powerful people on the planet as well — or so she thought.

Doubts would continually creep in. Maybe there was no way to stop him, not if he could make you forget yourself, forget him, make you lose yourself in realities that bore no similarity to what was really going on all around you.

Just how do you go about stopping a man like this?

It was clear that what Letje had believed she could do, that she could resist his influence, was a mistake, so she needed to come up with something that would ensure his demise in a way that allowed her to carry out such an act without him simply making her forget all about her plans, leaving herself wide open to attack, and death.

Arcene snored loudly, grunting as Leel turned to move her floppy ear away from the disturbance. Poor Arcene, yet how brave she was. She had been so sore Letje was amazed that she managed to walk as much as she did — being able to move at all after such a difficult birth was incredible, but walking such distances was not something Letje would have thought possible.

Yet Arcene did it, day after day. Resolute, serious; determined.

It wasn't only the drive to get her son back, although that was what made her do what she did, it was the power that sprang open like a cracked dam after she Awoke. In her despair, Arcene had gone deep and then deeper into The Noise, seeking out the information she needed, understanding in an instant how it was that you could alter your body and control anything to do with how it functioned.

It had take Letje a long time to understand such processes and there was more to learn, but Arcene's interest was limited in scope — she shut down the aging process, halted it forever, and understood how to repair the damage done to her from the birth. She finally managed to remove the terrible pain she felt every time she moved. She healed herself in less than a day, numbed the pain until she could feel normal again, and was obviously content that she would never again have to go through the terrible experience of laying with a man and having a child whether she wished to or not.

It was the most heart-rending thing Letje had ever experienced. Her friend had done something terrible to herself, all because she had been forced to become a woman before her time.

Letje settled down, hoping for a dreamless sleep, although the sky was already beginning to lighten and before long they would all be rising anyway, continuing their journey to take back their sanity from a man that had done much more than twist their minds: he'd twisted their hearts too. Letje knew that there were three woman more than happy to return the favor — happy to each twist a knife deep into his heart until he was dead and soon nobody would remember that such a man had ever lived. She just prayed it wasn't too late, that the damage he had done to the population wasn't irreversible.

What a stupid man. What use is a king without subjects to rule over?

A Morning Cuppa

Letje woke groggily, back stiff from yet another night sleeping on hard ground — perversely, the extended stay at Bridewell had made her body used to comfort, even if most of it was a blur. The fire was crackling away nicely though and she felt warm. Arcene and Leel were cuddled up tight, snoring fitfully, their favorite occupation.

Mother Superior passed her a steaming cup of tea and smiled, at least Letje thought it was a smile, it was hard to tell with those thin lips and devilish teeth.

"Surprise, that's what you need."

Letje didn't understand. "Surprise?"

Mother Superior nodded, while slowly, as she sipped on her tea, bits began to drift away from her head, tiny pieces just breaking loose and floating into the air as if she was nothing but ash, splintering apart as she cooled after being taken out of the fire.

Letje watched as more and more of Mother Superior dissipated, until all that remained of her head was her chin and mouth, those devilish teeth gleaming brightly as her lips drew back to blow on her tea before taking a loud slurp. Letje did the same, cupping her drink in both hands and sipping carefully at the piping hot beverage. She stayed calm, relaxed and thoughtful as she drank, watching Mother Superior slowly float off into the clear sky, dancing with the mist that was rising all around them as the heat of the day burned off the dew of the early morning.

When it was over, when there was nothing left but a half finished mug of tea placed carefully on the grass by the side of the fire, Letje turned her head slowly to check on what she knew she would see — Mother Superior, sat opposite her, staring into the flames, lost in thoughts of revenge, eyes bright and menacing. Letje got up, picked up the tea, and gave it to Mother Superior — she took it with a nod then drank without saying a word.

Easing out the stiffness from her limbs, Letje did a few stretches then returned to her makeshift bed and continued drinking even though it was now almost cold.

She had no idea who had made the tea, wasn't entirely convinced it was actually even real, but had decided that the best thing to do in these situations was go with it, not freak out, and soon enough the dream would pass and she would be back to her reality. At least, she tried to convince herself she came back to reality, there was no way of knowing really, all you could do was live in the world that your mind told you was the truth.

Since getting away from Bridewell, and the fog of Artek's manipulation finally lifted, Letje had been finding herself more and more confused by events happening all around her. It had got so that she found herself in strange places without knowing how she got there, or one minute she was having a conversation with Arcene only to discover she was actually talking to a rather confused and bored looked Leel. Or she was simply seeing things that were impossible, bits of her own body floating away — sometimes tiny pieces, sometimes large. One time she saw a whole foot just take to the air, sprouting tiny wings before disappearing into the clouds.

It was the after-effects of going into The Room For Dreams, she understood that after just a few days. With Artek's influence gone, and with her mind functioning normally once more, the effects of her adventures in the Room were once more taking hold and playing out in her mind with disturbing regularity. At first she had freaked out, feeling like she was going mad, or would do soon, until she realized that the only way to get through the terrible confusion was to accept it as if it were real then just carry on regardless. The result was that the dreams were becoming less and less disturbing. She was able to stay calm while they happened, and as she let them do what they would Letje came to realize that they were all leading up to something — trying to tell her something important. Finally it came.

As Letje sipped on her now cold drink, she felt a wave of clarity wash over her, the dream finally dissipating for good, leaving her back in her true reality as if she'd only been half there until now. The swirl of dream-lives still danced in the back of her mind, but it was unraveling, fading and leaving her, as if once accepted their job was done, the message given, so Letje could come back to herself, carry out the mission she had taken on, and succeed.

It all came down to one thing: surprise. The vision of Mother Superior actually speaking to her had been the catalyst for the end of the confusing dream-states she had been zoning in and out of for days now. The message was delivered. It was so simple, yet not something Letje had even considered. In her mind she had believed the confrontation with Artek would have to be head-on. A battle of wits and powers that would be terrible in its intensity and might well lead to her death, but the reality was that the best chance of actually dealing with such a man was to have the element of surprise, defeat him without him even knowing his end was due.

It felt like the coward's way, sneaking about and killing a man without him being able to fight back, but as she thought about it then such a demise made perfect sense. After all, wasn't that exactly how Artek treated people? Didn't he control their thoughts, stop them from remembering him, even kill them without them ever even knowing they were no longer of use to him?

It fit perfectly.

Now all Letje had to do was come up with some kind of a plan where they could get close enough to somehow eliminate him without putting themselves at risk, or endangering Arcene's baby and whoever else Artek happened to have with him now — if anyone.

Letje missed Gamm.

~~~

Day after day they walked, guided by the intensity of light emanating from Mother Superior's skin. Time became meaningless; they just walked. Mother Superior may have been small but she set a fierce pace, and by the end of the day all of them, apart from Leel, were exhausted, falling into a deep sleep before repeating the same thing the next day.

Letje felt herself becoming something else, something more than she had thought she was. It was as if the time she'd spent under Artek's spell was preparing her for the world that was to be her future. Now out from under his influence, and with the remains of the dream-state gone, Letje felt Awoken like she never had before. There were things taking shape within her that were both beautiful and terrible. It was terrifying and exciting.

She couldn't help think back to years ago when she had sat around a table with Marcus and Arcene and he had told of what it was to be him. At the time Letje had found it horrifying: the things he knew, could do and see, made him seem impossibly alien, living in a world not meant to be experienced by a mere human. But now Letje understood that such a future awaited her too, and with a clarity of mind that was finally unleashed she didn't know whether to accept such a responsibility and knowledge, or do whatever she could in her power to ensure such a life was never hers.

There was no choice, she had chosen her path long ago — chosen to Awaken and become something more, and now the truth of the choice was taking her over, exposing the world for her in ways she hadn't really believed possible.

Letje saw everything as it really was, as if her life had been a lie, the world hiding from her, never telling her the truth of what it was to really be a human being. She understood so much now, seeing everything through new eyes that were unaccustomed to the truth. As she sat staring at the fire in the evening, her companions each lost in their own thoughts, Letje could make sense of the flames. She understood the truth of such a complex number of chain reactions that allowed energy to be transformed but never die, all tied up into ever more esoteric systems that governed not only combustion and energy transfer, but how it equated to the rest of the planet, then out into the Universe, everything already there, nothing really changing in the end, just swapping states, becoming something else for a short period of time before returning to the nothingness that was all enduring. All that there had been, all that there would ever be.

She simply knew how reality functioned. She saw the fire and the knowledge went deep yet was instinctual. She understood how it worked, the mixture of gases that were needed for such a miracle to occur, the changing of the wood into flame as molecules danced ever faster, a cosmic vibration that played out in infinite ways throughout the Universe. She saw the ground beneath her feet for what it truly was: a complex ecosystem that could never be sustainable without millions of elements all coming together at the right time to allow it to thrive. From soil acidity to the need for worms and microbes, bacteria and countless other things she had no name for yet could 'see', knowing that each played a part, that each was as important as the next.

Trees danced in terrible complexity, leaves whipping as fast as a strobe light or moving as slowly as the cosmos. Time could be flashed through or taken as a snapshot, all of it there for her to know and understand on an intuitive level, not a knowledge gained by reading and learning, but real knowledge, 'knowing' things, understanding them. Seeing the consequence of a caterpillar chewing away on the fresh buds on the trees, the wind not catching those leaves that would have been, thus blowing differently across a tiny part of the countryside, taking a direction it never would have taken if the caterpillar hadn't taken its meal.

How each act had consequences rippling through time, making infinite futures play out in infinite universes through the smallest of acts — Fasolt's story of the ant played out forever in each and every single event that occurred at each and every point in time across universes that multiplied by the day, the hour, the second, the millisecond and down to where time had no meaning — it expanded, split in ways that allowed everything to happen somewhere, somehow.

It was easy to get lost in such knowledge, for what did one Letje matter when there were others living lives almost exactly the same as hers, completely different, and every degree in between? Yet it did matter, that was the whole point of such knowledge. Everything had a point, every thought, act, decision and movement had consequences and it was wise to consider how you acted, what you did with a life that was both absolutely meaningless and as important as anything else in the entire Universe she found herself, this self, making her way through precariously.

Such a responsibility was terrible; knowing so much an impossible burden. Such things she saw as she stared at the ground, understanding that with each step she took she changed the future of an entire universe forever in ways too subtle too imagine and in ways that could determine the path of her entire species. Letje became lost in it all, seeing madness beckon her with its infinite crooked finger. As she took a step, watching her foot land, she saw the future diverge across timelines, the placement of her step determining what would play out, what would have been different if she had landed just a fraction to the left or the right. She saw the fractured timelines, watched them spread and split in countless directions, following the paths down twisting, torturous routes that resulted in futures almost exactly the same, or futures that were so different to the one Letje lived in that it seemed impossible that a footfall could have such far reaching consequences.

In the end the only answer was acceptance. To let it all just play out in her mind, to watch herself watching such things as if she were an observer. Just standing in the shadows, a witness to what happened in her mind, not becoming an active participant, not taking on the responsibility of creating countless futures with every action.

There was no blame — there couldn't be, the only alternative was to never have existed at all. As Letje accepted the new insights and knowledge so it receded, not leaving, just moving to the back of her mind to become a permanent part of who she was now: a new her, reborn with the knowledge that everything meant the world even though it was all completely meaningless. And to try to change the future was a fool's errand — everything happened somewhere, so it meant little whether or not it happened in her insignificant timeline that this her just so happened to be making its way through. As each second brought about a different timeline, all of them diverging, some staying close others going off at impossible tangents, then the knowledge that truly there was no actual timeline for her meant that the responsibility was lifted. She walked through the future one step at a time, making her way as best she could, knowing that all possible futures were happening somewhere. In some the end for her was good, and in others it was very bad indeed — worse than she could have ever imagined.

So she didn't need to imagine, her Awoken state showed her it all, everything that could happen, everything that was happening, somewhere.

Letje did all that she needed to do — she watched her steps and watched futures spread out around her, lines diverging in all directions: in front, behind, up and down, into the sky, down into the earth. She followed the one that led her to a future that she wanted to play out for her, in this life, for the her that was thinking such thoughts, even though there were countless other hers thinking almost identical thoughts. It didn't matter, she knew who she was, this her here, thinking what she was thinking, the other hers would have to make their own way, follow their own footsteps, taking routes that led to a blissful future or one so tortuous she wondered how any of the countless hers could ever let such a future come to pass. But then, everything was possible so everything had to happen somewhere.

Just not here, not to me and my friends.

Letje wasn't expecting to have the opportunity to test out her new abilities quite as soon as she had to.

Arcene Returns

Arcene had been morphed from a girl full of life and vitality, naughty and curious, into a subdued and beaten woman. The spark was gone, the manic energy that drove her and made her do things she knew she shouldn't was replaced with a lassitude of the soul that threatened to shroud her in its cold embrace for eternity.

She was transformed since her ordeal into a broken woman — almost.

Letje could see the spark still inside of her, see it fighting for room to expand and engulf the young girl once more. There was nothing Letje could do — this was a battle of the spirit that Arcene had to overcome on her own. She had to fight her demons and come out victorious, so all that Letje could do was offer her support and be there for her friend. The final outcome was to be Arcene's and hers alone.

It was terrible to watch. To have to endure the misery that emanated from Arcene almost dragged

Letje down too. It was palpable, the only one seemingly inured was Mother Superior, who simply didn't care — she had her own world that she was firmly entrenched in and it consisted of her religious order and what had been done to it by Artek, nothing else mattered to her but revenge, then a resurrection of her previous life.

Arcene was broken, terribly lost, and Letje was unsure if she would ever be anything like the girl she had known before or if that child was now lost forever. Her innocence was certainly gone, never to be replaced. How could it be after the abrupt end of her childhood caused by a man that took her against her will and then compounded the injustice by taking the perfect child that was the result of such a terrible coupling?

She spoke little, was evasive and avoided eye contact most of the time, but what Letje found the most heart-wrenching of all was that Arcene wouldn't confide in her. Letje felt like a mother to Arcene so it broke her heart to know she was going through so much pain yet wouldn't, or couldn't, bring herself to talk it through with Letje. Arcene just couldn't face it, so Letje didn't push it.

Arcene's Awoken state was one that was centered around her internal abilities, ones she had used in such a dramatic fashion, and as far as Letje could tell that was to be where they stayed focused. It took so much energy to develop powers through The Noise and the severe halting of her body-clock, more dramatic that Letje had seen in anyone else, even herself or Marcus, meant that Arcene was unlikely to have a similar experience to her and in some way Letje knew it was for the best.

She couldn't imagine the outcome if Arcene ever came back to herself and became the mischievous girl she once was, then began entering the minds of other creatures — it would be chaos on a grand scale. She couldn't help smiling, imagining the mischief she would get up to if she was let loose on the animal population and decided to be a bear for a day or enter the mind of Leel — the two of them combined would send a shudder through the body of the strongest of warriors.

So day after day, as they followed the diminutive nun, Letje had to watch Arcene first sink deeper into despair but then, gradually, and to her immense relief, come out the other side — stronger, more powerful, more determined and laser-focused on her goal: getting her baby back.

It came to a head as they approached a steep gorge, a slice through the landscape that cut across the rough terrain, all loose scree and terrible paths, just goat trails that were so narrow they had to walk single file, making their way down the steep side, one hand touching the rock on their left for stability as they scrambled over boulders, constantly checking their footing on the sliding ground, praying no loud noise would disturb the loose shale above them.

Arcene was in front of Letje, Mother Superior leading the way, Leel at the rear, where Arcene had ordered her, there to keep guard and also keep her more subdued away from her mistress. Suddenly Letje realized that Arcene was back, maybe not back to how she was before, but there was something different — her body sparkled in The Noise like it used to, bright and mischievous, full to bursting, a strong life force that hinted at vitality and yes, naughtiness. Letje could see it if she looked in that certain way that was open to those that were Awoken; Arcene shone brighter than she ever had before.

It was because she was Awoken, but it was also as she had halted her body to forever be fifteen. It meant not only that she would look the same, but her hormonal level, and everything else, would remain stable and right for the girl of that age. Sure, her mind could mature and grow, but it wouldn't be the same as if her body aged too: the complex way a body worked was tied up with the brain developing, and with one halted then the way Arcene's mental faculties grew would also be different to if she aged normally.

It all combined to convince Letje that Arcene was fast recovering from her lassitude, almost as if she'd had The Lethargy. She could see it falling way, dead light in The Noise replaced with a shimmering that touched all around it and lit up The Noise.

Arcene was back.

Letje was focused on the tassel swishing on the hilt of Arcene's sword — something she had kept with her at all times since finding it at Bridewell before they left. Now it seemed to have a certain swagger to it, a pronounced swish that Letje realized was matched in Arcene's gait. It was the confidence of youth returned, Arcene awake to her surroundings and once more feeling invincible, ready to get 'deathy', which was just as well.

Arcene turned and smiled at Letje, a smile she hadn't seen for so long. It was as if her face became alive once more, and it brought memories flooding back to Letje, memories of Arcene stuck in strange contraptions, pulling levers and the ever familiar image of her eating, always hungry, as if her insides were hollow. Her eyes were still haunted though, skin sickly and hair lifeless in her now familiar pigtails. But she was back, Letje knew it, and so did Arcene. Leel picked up on it too, letting out a loud bark she tried to push past Letje, nearly knocking her off the narrow ledge to her death.

"Leel, no. You stay. Good girl."

Leel obeyed in an instant, sitting down right behind Letje, her breath tickling the back of Letje's neck as Leel panted heavily.

"Stupid dog," muttered Arcene, smiling at Letje.

"Hey," said Letje.

"Hey," said Arcene, both of them knowing that the worst was behind her, nothing more needing to be said. Arcene fumbled in a pocket then pulled out an acorn, smiling again at Letje, confirming their bond.

Letje nodded once more, trying not to let the tears flow.

"Boar," came the single word from Mother Superior, nothing more than a statement of fact.

Arcene turned, skirt swishing, tassel dancing wildly as the sword was pulled from the scabbard with a motion as fluid as water. Leel started growling and Letje had flashbacks to that awful day when Sy lost his life to one inhabited by the mind of an Eventual.

Mother Superior stepped back against the rock face, her tiny body almost disappearing into the stone as her habit blended so well with the gray shale. She seemed calm and totally relaxed, merely an observer in what was to play out, not threatened, confident that the animal would do them no harm.

It's going to kill us, we can't fight it on this ledge. Arcene's going to be first, she's already nearly on it and it isn't going to be happy.

Letje took one step forward and watched as an ever-expanding number of futures played out in an instant. All but one of them resulted in the death of all but Mother Superior — it seemed that this was not her day to die whatever future occurred. In each possible timeline she survived, some with her battered and bruised, but most with her unscathed, continuing her quest alone. The rest of the possible futures all saw Arcene, Letje and Leel dead, just in various orders and in various terrible ways. Letje took another step, as if in a dream, head spinning wildly with information overload that was out of time and space, an impossible volume of knowledge to filter all at once.

She saw it though, saw in a flash all the outcomes, recording each move they made, watching as each step, each shout or movement brought one specific future closer to being their reality in this universe.

There was a way to make it. Weaving through the myriad possible courses of action Letje watched one reality play out with minimal impact on other world events and with all of them surviving.

Letje halted the flow of time and took one step back, not physically taking it, but rewinding the clock for a heartbeat, stepping into her past to right the wrong that otherwise was committed with that forward motion. That split second had set them on a path that was impossible to escape, but if she took it back and let something different play out then they would be safe. She danced between the cracks in reality, took hold of her future and chose what it was to be.

The course was set now, there was no way to change what was about to happen — Letje had chosen the future for all of them.

She watched as Arcene moved forward, sword held high, ready to arc down and dispatch the beast, but it would be no good, she would find the sword stuck in a crevice in the rock wall, the boar gouging her from underneath as she crouched to try to pull the sword out. Letje knew what she had to do.

Letje put a foot out, spreading Arcene's legs a fraction. Her right foot slipped on the shale and Arcene slid over the side of the ledge. She dropped the sword and screamed as she began her descent. Letje made a dive for the floor just as the boar was upon them. It was huge, an ancient male with tusks as hard as iron, bristling with short fur standing on end like it had an electric shock. It was nothing but densely packed muscle, battle scars criss-crossing its hide like a history lesson in aggression. It snorted loudly, weighing up the people out of myopic eyes, pawing at the ground before it began to run right at them, gaining speed fast as it lowered its head, ready to gouge anything that stood in its path.

Letje watched it all in slow motion, reality taking on a clarity that allowed her to experience the odor of the boar, taste the fear in the air, and act calmly yet with lightning-fast reflexes. As Arcene's arms disappeared over the ledge, following her body, she reached out and grabbed hold of Arcene's wrist, lying prone on the ground, shale digging into her ribs. A split second later the boar ran right over her, hooves dancing in the air, jumping to avoid her body.

Leel seemed to understand the situation, looking around furtively for a way to avoid a collision, before copying Letje and simply laying down, legs sprawled out into the air, way too long to stay on the narrow path. The boar jumped the huge dog just as it had Letje, and in a second it was gone, only the clattering of its feet on the loose surface could be heard, echoing through the valley, before silence returned.

Easily coping with the weight of Arcene, Letje scrambled to her knees, stones as sharp as knives slicing through her clothes. She put a hand out and anchored it in a crevice in the rock and used the purchase to pull Arcene up slowly.

As she heaved on the arm Letje knew that Arcene was definitely back to being her old self as her head appeared over the ledge — a huge grin was spread wide across her face.

"That was a bit naughty Letje, you made me fall over."

"Haha, sorry about that. It was the only way we were going to get out of it alive, trust me on that."

"I trust you Letje, I trust you with my life," said Arcene, scrabbling at the ground then heaving her body back onto the path, arm reaching out for her sword, checking that Leel and even Mother superior were okay. "Leel, you can get up now. Good doggie."

Leel righted herself, looking rather embarrassed for not fighting, then walked over to Arcene and gave her a huge lick across the face while she was still lying on the ground defenseless. "Gee, thanks Leel."

Woof.

"I think we better run," said Letje.

"What? Why? It's gone hasn't it?"

"It has, but Leel's bark has just set off an avalanche," said Letje, looking up at the towering rock face that was crashing down toward them in a mess of loose shale and huge boulders.

"Mother Sup—" She was already gone, little legs kicking up splinters of rock as she ran for all she was worth away from the landslide that was going to be upon them in an instant.

She's not exactly a people person.

Letje heaved Arcene to her feet and they ran, Leel barking excitedly at whatever game it was they were now playing.

"Can you shut that dog up?" shouted Letje above the noise of the approaching rock.

"Why? She's having fun. C'mon, run faster. Faster!"

They ran as fast as they could, left arms trailing the rock for balance, as the cliff began to fall onto the path right behind them and tiny shards of death fell about them in all directions.

Not Just Any Bird

Son of Bird knew he was different to his brothers and sisters, he knew this as he was the only one that even had a concept of such a familial bond.

They were pure, free, unknowing and uncaring of the world around them. Son of Bird was different.

He knew he could have a name of his own if he wished, a name that only he and his father would ever know, but he liked the continuity, the taking of the name of what he understood to be the most powerful creature that had ever taken to the skies. Now it was his turn to marvel at a reality so few could ever witness. He became something more than just intelligent — as he grew to maturity he understood the gifts being given to him, and one day as he soared high, feeling the thermals, knowing the precise moment to tilt a wing to catch a hint of the change in the air and ride higher and higher, he truly Awoke to the knowledge only one other of his species had ever had the opportunity to witness.

It was then that he knew he should have a name of his own, that individuals should never be a clone of their parents, but should seek to forge their own path, to cherish family but also to think for himself, experience the world through his own eyes.

Bird, Son of Bird, became Demoulin.

Demoulin chose a name, chose a name from the memories of the people below, the people that allowed him to search their minds, take up residence for a short period of time just as they themselves had entered the minds of animals. Demoulin knew that his father had decided to remain simply Bird, a name signifying the first of what amounted to a new species. Now it was time for the lineage to progress, for their importance to be recognized as the skies would soon be full of Awoken ones from the line begun by his father and his mother. But Demoulin was the first of the new order that would expand above the rooftops of The Commorancy, the collection of what he understood to be a form of nest for the humans, the strange creatures that would forever be bound together with his kind — a symbiosis that would benefit both as long as there was the appropriate respect.

With vast knowledge came the burden of responsibility: for his family and for the world he now lived in. He was given insight from the man known as Marcus, his experiences shared, and also those of his father, telling him of the strange games played by man, their kindness and their cruelty, their sadness and happiness.

Demoulin accepted it all, his awareness expanding with the knowledge, and he went to seek out the one known as Letje, the female at the heart of the countless possible futures he saw spreading out in all directions via his insight into The Noise. Paths countless in number, but so very fragile, many of them leading to nothing but emptiness.

Yet there were certain timelines that promised greatness for not only the line begun by Bird but for the future of the species he couldn't help but feel sorry for. Demoulin went to help; he had chosen the path he wished to see come to fruition, bonding forever the two disparate creatures known as bird and human.

~~~

Letje felt the presence approach, her mind shooting up into the sky like an arrow: straight and true, her consciousness gladly accepted as the creature's first sentient passenger, then the greeting was over, vast knowledge shared outside of time and place.

Standing on the top of the cliff, on the other side of the gorge they had barely escaped from with their lives, it already felt like days ago that it had happened. The truth was it was merely a matter of hours, but with Arcene fully back in the present, the new reality Letje was aware of, and the knowledge she now had, it felt like lifetimes had passed, not just a few hours carefully traversing the valley floor, deep in shadow and cold, before emerging without incident up the other side into the open skies and the cool wind that blew away the past, sweeping them towards the future.

The air parted as Letje welcomed her new friend onto her dead shoulder. She smiled sweetly as Demoulin gently teased her earlobe. It made her realize just how much she had missed Bird — he'd left shortly after his arrival, vanishing without trace.

"Hello my friend. Demoulin, such a lovely name."

He turned his head to face her, staring into eyes newly Awoken to the true potentials of the Universe, and let out a *screeee* so loud that Letje jumped despite herself.

"Haha, I couldn't agree more my young friend. Going to give your father some time to himself are you? Have some adventures of your own?"

Demoulin blinked rapidly, taking in the feel of his new friend, and found that he was happy with the woman. He took to the air, then swooped down and landed on the back of Leel, who uncharacteristically didn't jump around wildly or try to attack the bird, but seemed almost as if she was waiting for such a strange companion to complete the group.

Arcene looked on with wide eyes, knowing that such a passenger was right. Mother Superior gave the bird nothing but a perfunctory glance then paid it no more attention.

They began walking once more, the huge eagle hitching a ride on the back of the equally oversized Leel. A strange sight, if there had been anyone else to see, but there wasn't, and to those in the group it seemed like the most natural thing in the world.

Energy crackled and radiated around the small company as knowledge was exchanged, power combined, future paths explored. Even Mother Superior allowed her closed-off knowledge to be shared in part: a life so strange, her interests so esoteric that even to Demoulin it was a little too bizarre to be anything more than a curiosity.

Letje delved deep into the exchange, aware that there was much more to the ancient woman than met the eye.

An Extra Pair of Eyes

Not wanting to pry, Letje noted that Demoulin and Mother Superior were now often communing via The Noise, but took it no further than that, giving them their privacy. The huge, still somewhat immature eagle, mostly rode on Leel, the dog seemingly fine as long as there were minimal piercings of her skin from the huge talons. When Demoulin had come in fast for landing and blood had bubbled to the surface, staining her coat, she had run around howling and crying for so long that Demoulin was careful from then on, landing as softly as a feather on lush grass.

This seemed to satisfy Leel, and they became almost constant companions for much of each day. But then he would take to the skies, exploring the way ahead, reporting back to Letje about what he saw, getting more information from Mother Superior. So the search continued, hope growing greater as the distance between them and their quarry lessened in equal measure.

When Leel wasn't rather stoically transporting live cargo — a job she seemed to take very seriously — her and Arcene bonded as if for the first time. They played, they ran and they rolled around on the ground like two small children. Which is how Letje thought of them again, inordinately happy to see her friend back to her almost usual fun-loving self.

Leel was gaining in confidence too — being back out in the open skies had seen her rather subdued, partly due to Arcene seemingly lost to herself, partly due to the overwhelming plethora of all the countryside had to offer. But as she got braver, and her curiosity had been satisfied once more, she was truly coming into her own. She warned of danger, both real and imagined, often emerging from a bush or a thicket with a rabbit, a squirrel, and most eagerly anticipated of all, a pheasant — meat they had all grown to love if for no other reason than the fact that it definitely didn't taste of chicken, which so much other meat did.

Yet however jolly a few hours might be, always looming over them was the theft of Arcene's child, the leaving of Artek, and the terrible piles of bodies he had left in his wake. Letje had no doubt that the man was a complete and utter maniac, somebody that was extremely dangerous and more powerful than she could have ever imagined.

She felt no fear, only a dogged determination to see events through to the end, following timelines as carefully as a child taking its first steps, watching each tiny event unfold, ensuring that it made the correct ripples through The Noise, that she was keeping them all on one of the few paths that saw a future for herself, her friends and companions, and for humanity as a whole. No easy task for somebody only recently aware of exactly what was possible for the human mind to understand.

Not only that, but to manipulate and play in the cracks between reality made a mockery of how she had been taught the world functioned. She had known of the powers hidden from her, but had never truly understood the knowledge Marcus had gained. Now she knew; it was a scary prospect.

Sad too. She had thought her innocence lost once before, when she Awoke, but that was as nothing to the true Awakening she had not long ago experienced, fully understanding the responsibility, the powers in constant turmoil all around her, ever changing but a constant, a flux that finally only ever led to one outcome: everything returned to The Void sooner or later.

Letje fought countless inner battles as they made their way toward Artek, trying to cope with the new insights into the world that were opening up to her almost constantly, battling to stay on top of knowledge and not let it swallow her up, succumbing to the realization of how blinkered she and the rest of humanity really were concerning the world they lived in.

It made her more determined than ever that Artek would never obliterate the remaining population. What the world offered them was simply too beautiful and terrible in its scope for humanity to not be allowed to experience it for themselves.

~~~

Days passed; each worse than the last. Try as she might Letje saw no signs of life, even when reaching deep into The Void, searching for people to help fill the emptiness that crept across the country like a dark, desolate stain. There was nothing.

They settled into a routine with their new friend. Mother Superior took to walking beside Leel, communing grim-faced, teeth shining in the light, taking no more than ten minutes before resuming her place at the front of the group once more, checking her Ink, fine-tuning their direction. Demoulin would then take flight, appear later in the day, report to both Letje and Mother Superior before then disappearing again until the following morning. He had much to explore, Letje knew, but he became a true friend, and took the place of his father on Letje's shoulder every day, if sometimes only for a quick nuzzle of her ear.

Arcene began to get extremely agitated, burning off nervous energy through rough play with Leel, who reveled in the craziness as much as her mistress. But there was a darker side to the play, Letje could see it. It was like watching young animals tumbling with their brethren to learn the skills for catching their own prey once they were older. The energy built and built; Arcene was clearly itching to come face to face with the man that had caused so much pain, to her more than anyone else.

Every day they walked, the miles now meaningless, their muscles accustomed to such daily punishment. They passed through woods, they skirted long collapsed towns and passed directly through countless small villages, now little more than collections of rubble, the buildings finally succumbing to the gradual erosion of the ever-encroaching plants that grew in crevices, pulling apart the bricks and the concrete little by little until it all came tumbling down, creating new homes for the animals that now lived contentedly where once their ancestors feared to venture.

They saw nobody. Not a single person was evident, not even with the explorations of Demoulin. The landscape was as devoid of human life as it was abundant with animals. Artek had worked long and hard scouring the land for people, eliminating many where he found them, taking others with him to build his new world how he saw fit, many of them dying of old age or infirmity before he had even made a decision concerning where his seat of power was to truly be.

Others were killed in much more terrible ways — the slightest hint of failure to accept Artek meaning their death was often slow and terrible.

At night they camped in the open, warmed by the fire, staring into the flames, each lost in their own visions of what they saw dancing in its searing heart.

Letje saw only one thing: the face of Artek. Orange hair, confident smile, features she hated more than anything and would see wiped from the surface of the planet if it was the last thing she ever did.

They were getting close, Letje knew it as well as the others did. All they had to do was keep walking and make sure that when they met Artek there was no way that he would be able to influence them, make them forget themselves, forget him, and wonder what they were doing standing before a strange man before he put an end to their lives without them even knowing why.

Letje knew what she had to do.

Me First

"I want to do it, I want to be the one that rips his smug head off. No, actually I'll do it with this, I'll chop it clean off." Arcene swung the sword around wildly, showing off moves she had perfected by practicing daily since she came back to herself.

Letje sighed, going over the same argument they had been having for days now. "Arcene, how are you going to do it? We've talked about this. If you are close enough to chop his head off then you're close enough for him to make you forget you even know him, or that you have a baby." Arcene's defiant stare lost its intensity and she hung her head, hair spilling across her face, hiding the tears. "I'm sorry, I'm sorry. I know it's hard, but we have to ensure nothing goes wrong. Come here."

Letje eased Leel to the side, the dog trying to comfort Arcene by rubbing her head against Arcene's side, and she gave her a tight yet cautious hug, keeping one eye on the sword.

"Okay Letje, I'll do as you say. But this can't go wrong, it simply can't. We have to get my boy back. I want to see him, give him a name, know what he should be called. But how can I do that when I don't even know what he looks like, not really?" Arcene began to sob again, Letje's heart breaking into pieces once more. Arcene wasn't equipped to deal with the loss of a child, she was still one herself, always would be.

"Hush, we'll get him back, don't you worry. And I will kill him. We'll end this; we will get Gamm too, get everyone that is left and make it alright again."

Mother Superior watched stoically, saying nothing, just staring at her Ink, watching the blue pulse rhythmically, the color getting brighter. She smiled, teeth glinting orange from the fire that was spitting fat as the rabbits cooked over the flames.

~~~

They were close now, Letje could feel it, knew it without being told by Demoulin, without looking at the pulsing Ink of Mother Superior. Life opened to her in new ways; everything was there for the knowing if she wanted it. She had only one thing on her mind: Artek.

The world vibrated for Letje, everything lit up, transparent, the sap visibly flowing through the trees, immense pressures in the trunk contained by the life-force within. She could see it all, the connections between every single thing on the planet, how she was at the epicenter of it all, her decisions and her future linked to the course of history for everyone and everything else. Reality shone in all its glory, layer after complex layer all now opened to her, telling tales of impossibly complex systems, how everything relied on everything else. Letje followed the path that weaved through the future, making certain with every heartbeat that she kept to the right path, trying not to get lost in the fact that she had in one respect already lived the future yet had to live it again to ensure it actually happened.

This was the madness that Marcus had warned about — making it hard to live in the present or to even care about what you did when you had already seen the future, experienced it, making reality lose its meaning. It was easy to get lost to insanity. She held fast, kept to the present, not letting the future overwhelm her, fighting against the after-effects of her deep dreaming that led to the discovery of Marcus, the true Marcus.

It was hard to accept the fact that they had found him, and however much Marcus insisted he was truly the original there was a nagging suspicion at the back of her mind that there was more to come, new surprises, new Marcus' to uncover in the seemingly endless complex that was The Commorancy.

Letje lay back on the grass, reveling in a rare period of peace and quiet, time to be alone. Arcene and

Leel were dozing in the shade after devouring their meal as if it was the first they'd had in days, and Mother Superior was off on her own as was her usual way when not eating, which they all always did together.

Reaching out, she was gladly accepted to share the sights witnessed by Demoulin, who was now a few days walk ahead of them, watching cautiously as the caravan of people and horses wound their way toward their final destination. Letje felt Artek's presence below, the insanity radiating off him in fierce burnt orange sparks, and she sensed Gamm too, lost in a haze of forgetfulness, putting one foot in front of another, neither knowing or caring about his situation. There were others too, minds she could sense, some more aware than the rest, all of them under Artek's control to a greater or lesser degree. Some were conforming because they had little choice, others because they knew no different. She also sensed a familiar mind, that of a man trapped in the body of a horse: Ahebban.

Delving deeper, feeling his predicament through The Noise, Letje read the history of the mind, understanding that he was acting as a beast of burden because he had little choice. Here was an ally, someone that could help when the time was right, so Letje reached out to him tentatively, her mind connecting carefully to his, reaching down from Demoulin, making a link that she would have thought impossible before she truly came to understand the very fabric of the world and how she was now something so different to the rest of the population.

It was unnerving. She felt like a goddess; a magical being that could perform tricks that went beyond the logic of the Universe and allowed her to pass through the very nature of things and perform feats that would seem impossible to all but a handful of enlightened souls.

The new knowledge scared her. Letje understood that she was gaining access to something that nobody should have access to: The Void. The everything and the nothing that was at the heart of all realities, the place where it all began and it all ended yet never ended. The only thing that endured for eternity, in constant flux yet as static and ageless as reality itself.

She was a part of it, could sense vast minds on the periphery, ancient beings waiting their turn to be reborn in one of countless forms. There was sentience of all description: huge and small, the constant passing through of energy that held no regard for time, reconfigured in the past, the present and the future on countless worlds as creatures as varied as there were stars in the universes. The energy that formed everything was partially opened to her, allowing Letje to manipulate her world in ways that put her apart from any other person that had ever been, elevating her to a level that was terrifying — for with such power came an immense responsibility.

Letje snapped out of it, fearing for her sanity after seeing what was never supposed to be accessed by the minds of humans while still alive. Much of her wished she could go back to being the girl that she used to be, the one that lived at home and knew nothing of the immense powers at work in the Universe that could rip apart her mind like little more than a cosmic hiccup.

She missed her father, feeling guilty for not having thought of him much lately, caught up in events that didn't allow her to take time for personal reflection of such a painful type.

What must this be like for Marcus? How can he cope with such things?

But that wasn't the problem, was it? Had Marcus really coped or had he lost his mind long ago? Letje felt it was best not to dwell on it for too long, she had to hold on to her sanity, not let her new reality overwhelm her and leave her old self far behind. She must cling to her humanity, her young self, stay grounded and behave as she should.

Sorry Daddy, I still love you, and I always will. Letje smiled at the memory of him as a tortoise — what a truly bizarre world she found herself living in. Wondrous too.

Part of her wanted to give up fully to it all, let the immense energy of the Universe flow through her and become elevated to something that would hardly resemble a human being any longer. Just to know, just to finally know what it was that was possible. This was what The Lethargy was all about, she was sure of it now: to force sentient species to finally become what they were meant to be, take their place in the Universe truly understanding the immense powers that swirled around and through them constantly, experience the true nature of reality and marvel at the opportunity to be alive in the first place — something so rare it was next to impossible.

"I see you," said Mother Superior. "I see what you are, my Sister."

Letje shielded her eyes and stared at her, huge head looking even more distorted from Letje's position on the ground. She got to her knees and stared at the old woman, really, truly seeing her for the first time. "I see you too... Sister."

No more words were spoken, the two women had no need for them. They stared at each other, each seeing the truth behind the flesh. Letje saw Mother Superior for what she genuinely was: an incredibly powerful woman, full to the brim of strange energy, the force of The Noise flowing through her Ink, swirling around the complex patterns, dancing at the chance to be unleashed. There were many more once hidden depths to the strange woman — she may have lived in isolation but there was no denying that she was immensely powerful. She simply chose a different path through life, and Letje was certainly in no position to judge her, after all, look at where she had decided to call home.

Then it was over, the knowledge of each other shared, a connection made, acknowledgment of each other as equals. The first time Mother Superior had ever deigned to accept another as such.

"Hey, anything to eat?" asked Arcene sleepily, wandering back to the fire, rubbing away the sleep from the eyes.

Leel wagged excitedly beside her.

Letje shook her head in wonder; they really were made for each other.

Mother Superior just stared at the pair blankly — she really didn't seem to find much amusing.

Almost Home

Artek felt strange. Somehow he found the knowledge that his mother was gone comforting. There was a freedom that he had never felt before and it brought the whole world to life. It was as if now the maternal bond was severed he was able to truly experience the world and his heart sang with the freedom he now had, the ability to do whatever it was he wanted without having to have that knot of dread in his stomach because his mother might disapprove.

It had been ridiculous and he knew it — a man of his age still tied to his mother, letting her run his life, direct everything from the way he acted to how and what he ate. Now he was as free as the horse beneath him once was, and his spirit lifted at what was to come, the life he would finally be able to lead.

Yet at the same time there was, if not fear, then something that came very close — for now his destiny lay firmly in his own hands. He was responsible and there would be nobody else to blame if it all went wrong. He turned and looked at the long line behind him, not as many subjects as he had hoped to start his reign with but it would suffice. It would only grow stronger year upon year.

He shook his head, red hair swaying, still amazed at just how few worthwhile people there were in the country. Over the years he had sought out them all, eliminating some on the spot as soon as he met them, seeing them for what they really were, knowing they would be useless in the future he had planned for himself and his lineage. How could so many of the remaining population be such a waste of space? Didn't they know they were supposed to grow as a person, be something?

But then, he supposed that was why he was who he was and they were what they were: King and subjects. It was actually rather sad to finally understand that most people had little to no aspirations and they just wanted to live their lives quietly — the most they aspired to was having plenty of food, somewhere nice and warm to live, and a family. He wanted a family too, his mother had certainly been right about the importance of continuing the family line, but he had plans, dreams and goals that he would allow nothing to stand in the way of.

He looked from face to face of those behind him, some on horseback, others in ancient wooden caravans known as vardo, drawn by stronger breeds of horse, plus many on foot. Staring at them, looking into their

241

minds as if they were open books, he read their past, pulling it directly out of their heads, nodding each time his decision to keep them alive was confirmed by what he saw.

This was the best he could do, the best people left in the country. He'd kept either those that were intelligent but he could still easily control, or those that were relatively weak of mind so would be perfect as the working class, tending the fields, serving him and his new family. There were also women that he found beautiful and now would make up his harem, replacing Arcene, that disappointment that he still felt rather foolish for falling for.

And Awoken, many were Awoken. It was inevitable: he'd been taking people for so long that many with normal lifespans simply grew too old to be of use any longer.

All of it would be for him, and his son, and they would rule together as King and Prince, increasing the population through the subservient but beautiful women they would surround themselves with, dominating the country before spreading around the globe until the world was theirs and every person submitted to their rule — or paid the price.

All that was now left was to actually begin.

Turning in the saddle to face the front Artek shielded his eyes against the sun and thought he caught sight of his new home for the first time in many years. This was his, a home he had kept secret from his mother so she couldn't interfere, and a place he had spend a relatively large amount of time and energy getting right over the years as and when he was able. There had been sacrifices, not for him but for those that had helped to get The Castle just right, up to his standards and ready for occupancy when he found the time right. That time was now.

A few more days and they would arrive. Then he could finally set things in motion, ensuring that life ran smoothly and he could maybe even take a rest from the control he had to continually exert to keep people in their place. That would be nice, not having to constantly influence the minds of his people, to relax, enjoy it, let them get to their work, begin the tending of the countryside, plowing the fields, repairing the buildings that would be their homes and the homes of their families.

Initially he thought he would keep things rather contained, just a few miles surrounding the vast complex that was The Castle, housing his immediate retainers within the walls, gathering in more and more cattle. He had gone to great pains to have them herded into enclosed areas over large swathes of the countryside ready to be brought by his servants so they could expand milk, meat and dairy production to start transforming the country into the beginnings of an Empire. One that would be ruled with an iron fist but with leniency as long as everybody knew their place, understood that they were ruled but looked after, had plenty of food, bore children that were Whole, healthy and would one day Awaken.

He smiled at the thought of what he would create, of all that had been done so far to get to this point. The years of hardship, his constant traveling, sifting through the dregs of humanity trying to find those worthy and those that he could watch through The Noise and know for sure wouldn't be a drain on resources; people with skills, those that would remain Whole, and those that would bow to his will and be happy with their lot.

It hadn't been easy but here he was, son in his arms for a short spell before he gave him back to the wet nurse, the beginnings of the new order now set into motion.

All that was left was to deal with those that were following him. His final game, one he could have dealt with back at Bridewell, but he had decided to let them live, just to see quite how persistent they would be. They might be of use after all if they proved themselves worthy, the only thing he was a little surprised at was that the nun had survived, and he was infinitely pleased about that. She had a lot of knowledge, and once he had her then he intended to strip her mind bare, take all she knew, then maybe he would allow her to live, to head a new religion, one that dispensed with all the mumbo jumbo and had a proper figurehead, a real living God to worship: King Artek.

Yes, that was it. Why not? After all, wasn't he the one that was to save the country? Not Marcus with his damn Commorancy, but him, the man that had cleaned up the mess caused by The Lethargy, eradicating it almost entirely by getting rid of the inferior of their species, beginning again as it should be, with only the best surviving, able to transform the country through the force of his will.

Artek smiled broadly, he would be King and God. People would fear him, worship him, and he would rule for thousands of years with his son by his side — they would be invincible, but kind. You had to be kind too. After all, you wanted your subjects to love you as well, didn't you?

A Sacrifice

Ahebban felt the change in Artek, felt his mood lighten, the jabs in his flanks becoming gentler, and he could see why. Up ahead, probably only a morning's trek away, was a huge castle set in the middle of acres and acres of pasture land, animals of all description fenced into separate enclosures, feeding on the grass, keeping it as short as a well maintained lawn.

There were people there, hard at work, fixing the fencing, hammering away at new posts to increase the acreage, and dominating everything else was the huge stone edifice of a castle that was clearly built long ago, easily withstanding the test of time. Built to last, this was once the seat of power of somebody that had clearly been wealthy, and it showed. Ahebban could see that as well as the castle proper, with huge crenelated tops that would give a clear view for miles in all directions, there were numerous additions, large and small, and outer courtyards complete with buildings he didn't doubt contained quarters for servants as well as stables for the horses and other animals that could be kept within the walls in case of siege.

Not that there was any chance of a siege nowadays. Artek had put a stop to any risk of that happening. It still seemed impossible, that one man could wreak such havoc, but it just goes to show that being Awoken really did change humanity. Why, he only had to consider his own situation to know it to be the truth. After all, here he was, once a man, now a horse and being degraded by carrying this crazed individual on his back.

No matter, soon it would all be over. Maybe then finally humanity would have a chance.

~~~

They made their way at a good pace toward the new base of power, Artek's excitement building as he shouted out orders. The few men he trusted enough they weren't held against their will were rallying around, directing those in a stupor, goading those that were lagging behind, slapping Ahebban's extended family on the flanks to get them to speed up even though the frothing at their mouths was a clear sign they needed rest, water and cooling down.

The sun beat down fiercely. Ahebban could feel the heat radiating off his body, steam rising like a boiling cauldron mixing with the air, flies gathering to take advantage of the moisture on offer.

None of it mattered, soon it would be over. Soon there would a reckoning and he would have to try to come to terms with the part he played in the destruction of all he held dear.

It hadn't been so bad anyway, life as a horse had given him a freedom from the constraints of a human body he never could have imagined. The things he'd seen, the things he'd done — there was no describing the freedom you felt running through the countryside on four strong legs, the wind blowing your mane, knowing that you were truly a part of the natural order, even if it had been achieved by rather unconventional means.

This wasn't the end anyway, just another change, a chance to do something good and to be a part of the next stage of evolution.

Ahebban couldn't wait.

Extreme Omnisience

Marcus was in The All-Seeing Room. A Room he had never truly taken advantage of as, if he was honest, it scared him. Marcus wasn't scared of anything apart from one thing: losing his sanity.

He knew that he was far from being a normal man, and would be classed as eccentric by any standards, but he felt that he still had a tight grip on his mind and unless he really had traveled so far down the rabbit hole of madness that he couldn't see the truth before him, then he truly did believe he was still sane.

Sort of.

Entering a Room such as this put it all in jeopardy, yet he had to know, he simply had to.

The outfit he wore had been picked out very carefully for such a solemn and dangerous undertaking, and he was rather pleased with his choice. For such a momentous undertaking he had chosen what at first seemed like a rather eclectic mix of items, but they all came together to create an ensemble piece that he was inordinately pleased with.

He wore a brown felt hat that had a history dating back to the frontier days in the American mid-west, worn by one of the many outlaws that later became immortalized by the press. He wore a striking pale blue paisley shirt combined with leather trousers and a brown belt, all set off with a rather dashing neckerchief and a pair of thin leather boots that fit him like a glove. He was tempted to wear spurs but thought that going a little too far, so instead had settled for a splash of silver with a belt buckle depicting the endless battle of good and evil in the stylized form of the yin/yang symbol.

All thought of his appearance soon vanished as he closed the door to the Room and took his seat in one of the more bizarre contraptions The Commorancy contained. He couldn't help smiling at the thought, as he truly did have some very strange pieces of machinery, functional and abstract.

This was different.

This was a chair for a state of mind. Not a chair that would hook him up directly to the scenes he wished to witness and feel a part of, no, this was intended to allow him to enter a special place, a place where everything and nothing resided for eternity. Marcus was going to watch the beginning of a new reality from the periphery of The Void — the most dangerous undertaking known to man.

He had sampled The Void on many occasions, impossible for nearly every other person on the planet, but he had done it nonetheless — witnessed incredible events, seen the very fabric of reality and what it held. Now he was going to go deeper, search out and watch the events that were soon to occur, but may as well have happened millennia ago for all it mattered in The Void, where everything that would happen and had happened played out simultaneously with no regard to the feeble invention of conscious minds that was called time.

Marcus settled back into the deep confines of the chair, let himself drift away from his body as he sank deeper, paying no mind as he spun around the room in an abstract pattern mimicking the dance of quarks through space and time until he was no longer in the past, present or future. He was everywhere and nowhere; he could witness everything that ever had been and ever would be, if he dared, but that way he knew madness waited, so he limited himself to a tiny portion of the globe where he could watch as if from the heavens, experience as if he was in the minds of those that played their games below, and feel the conflicting emotions that spilled out into The Noise, causing countless realities to be born and die in the blink of a cosmic eye.

Marcus was God, if for just a moment.

When Gods Collide

Letje had done all that she could, mentally preparing herself, physically priming her body for what was to come. Demoulin sat on her shoulder, nuzzling at her earlobe, telling her the last of what she needed to know.

Mother Superior was as stoic as ever, but Letje was sure there was a hint of a smile beneath her dour countenance.

Probably looking forward to getting her revenge.

Arcene and Leel were practically brimming over with nervous energy, as excitable as two puppies let loose in the world for the first time. Arcene was fervently practicing her various moves, and even Leel knew to stay well clear of the flashing steel that arced through the air in crazy combinations too fast for the human or animal eye to see unless like Letje you had the ability to calculate the movements before Arcene herself even began her stroke.

It was time. Finally there would be a reckoning for what Artek had done.

~~~

They crested the rise of the gently sloping land, the vista opening up behind them, clear and rugged, swept by a regular easterly wind that stunted the growth of the native trees and rippled across the grass like invisible serpents. Then Letje looked forward toward their ultimate goal, their quarry in the distance, heading toward the magnificent castle, a fortification Letje would do her utmost to ensure never became the seat of power for a madman.

The minds in front of her radiated an almost empty silver in The Noise, devoid of that true spark of life that signaled independent thought, freedom and the ability to act for oneself unhindered. Yet some were clearly free to do as they chose, and were reveling in the opportunity to be a part of what Artek promised. These were the most depraved of people as far as Letje was concerned, their happiness based on the misery of others, just there as playthings to be dominated and manipulated for their own satisfaction — when they should be trying to rebuild all that had been lost by people that truly cared for others and wanted everyone to flourish.

At the spearhead of the group was Artek, coat flapping in the wind, red hair shining like a beacon of fire, power radiating off him in pulses of sickening green just like his shirt.

Letje nodded; the plan went into action as the very fabric of reality ripped apart and minds screamed at what she was about to do, minds that watched from miles away yet truly watched from that impossible vantage point: The Void.

Thunder ripped through reality as energies were mutated and her warning cry rang out across the landscape, scaring the animals in the fields and startling the horses out of their stupor, sending them rearing on hind legs, shaking their heads, manes tumbling in the air wildly. Reality came crashing back for them and immediately they yearned for their freedom, intent on making their escape, returning to the tranquil lives they had once known yet had forgotten were still theirs for the taking.

Letje could see Artek lift his head to look at the skies, trying at the same time to control Ahebban.

Now, do it now.

Ahebban responded to Letje's instructions through The Noise, and before Artek could clutch his mind in his vice-like grip Ahebban released his consciousness from the home he had enjoyed for so long and his very being leapt into the ether, shooting as fast as a fallen star directly into a young male's mind, a brother to Demoulin, Son of Bird.

Ahebban looked down from his new home, watching as his old body collapsed to one side, Artek still in the saddle. He soared effortlessly, his part in the fight done, and began to get to know his host.

Down below on a tiny patch of earth on the vast planet chaos reigned as Artek crashed to the ground, the weight of the now dead huge horse pinning a leg as Letje, Arcene, Leel and Mother Superior ran toward him across the wind-swept fields. People and horses were running in all directions, their minds freed for a moment as Artek lost his hold on them. Letje could see Gamm trembling much like the others were, suddenly confronted with a reality he didn't understand, unknowing of how he got where he was, trying to make sense of his situation.

Then he was still, and Letje watched in dismay as he walked over to where Artek was trapped and heaved at the corpse of the horse. It shifted slightly and Artek scrambled to his feet, face as red as his hair, brushing at his clothes, frantically patting his hair back into place as if all that was happening was that his wardrobe had got a little messy.

As Letje and the rest of her party got closer it was clear that the spell of freedom for those with Artek was well and truly over. They were still, docile and as vacant as those in the grips of The Lethargy. She had hoped that the fall would have caused him serious damage, the sacrifice of Ahebban more effective, but no matter, she would do what she had to do, ensure he never got to have the baby again.

The child was clutched tightly by the wet nurse, wrapped up tight against the wind, so Letje knew that at least he was safe — Artek would never risk the life of his own child, she knew that much about the man. Letje tore through reality into the future, watching timelines converge then split, echoes ringing back to the past, to her current time, countless choices viewed, weighed up against the other like a chess master, before she was sure once more what had to be done.

They were getting close now, close enough to Artek to see his features, the scowl that spread across his face as he looked at them, then the muscles relaxing into a smile, the utter confidence returning as he brushed at his shoulder and spread his arms wide as if in invitation for Letje to try to stop him. She saw the confidence, knew he believed that with his power he could simply shut them all down, make them forget he'd ever existed, leave them standing there as defenseless as Arcene's baby, for him to do with as he wished.

He's going to regret his confidence, I'll see to that.

Letje was firmly back in the present, yet she could see the timelines spread out in all directions. All she had to do was follow the one that allowed them to live, to overcome. She nodded to Mother Superior, who smiled wickedly, pulling back her makeshift cornette, letting her gray hair flow freely in the wind. The strange woman then pulled her habit over her head, as if wanting to savor the release of her hair before doing so, and then there she was, a strange little naked woman, body of a child, large head and filed teeth, covered head to toe in intricate swirls of raised Ink, pulsing with an inner blue light that strobed through the air, making it pulse with the rhythm of a thousand drums, *boom, boom, booming,* sending shockwaves rippling through the air and the ground, the grass flattening, matching the patterns on her body, pushing back the wind and the very fabric of reality, mesmerizing Letje with their beauty and their terrible inner power.

The pulsing hit Gamm like a physical blow to the head, and he clutched his skull, wailing just like every other person apart from Letje and Artek. Then he relaxed, staring around as if seeing his situation for the first time, before everything came flooding back to him and he ran the short distance between himself and Artek, slamming into the man's side, sending him hurtling through the air before crashing hard to the ground once more.

The pulsing slowed in intensity and Mother Superior ran screaming across the space between them and Artek, a wild, primeval scream of anguish for the abuse Artek had dished out, the death he had been a part of, a wail of pure revenge for the death of her Sisters, the ruination of her Order: a way of life for over three hundred years. It would have been funny, Letje couldn't help note as she stared at the wrinkled behind of Mother Superior, if it wasn't for the fact that she knew the small woman had every intention of ripping out Artek's throat with her teeth as soon as she possibly could.

Arcene and Leel, now free from the all-encompassing immobilizing effects of Mother Superior's Ink, were tearing across the gap toward Artek, Leel loping easily beside Arcene, keeping enough distance so that Arcene's sword, wielded high but already descending for a death blow as she overtook Mother Superior, didn't catch her before it met its victim. It was no good, Letje knew, but it had to play out like this, and so she ran toward her friends and her enemies, each step placed precisely, keeping to the timeline, knowing it was happening as it should.

Events unfolded as she knew they would, Artek tumbling away from Gamm, pulling the large man expertly into his place as he rolled away, Arcene's sword descending in an arc that would see Gamm's head split in two, brains spilling into the blunt grass.

A Meeting of Minds

Marcus' mind expanded to fill a tiny corner of The Void, clinging to his sanity as it tried to take him in, make him a true part of the emptiness, bring him back where he belonged. He resisted; he watched the battle for humanity's future play out.

~~~

Letje sank deep into The Noise in an instant, stepping forward between the cracks in time, and as she watched Arcene's sword descend in slow motion she grabbed hold of the slender shoulders of her friend and adjusted her position slightly to the left before walking over to Artek, pulling her dagger from her side, and mischievously slicing half of his fringe away, lifting the hair to in front of his face, letting go and watching it ever so slowly begin to descend. She stepped back out of harms way, checking that she had the space that she needed, receding from The Noise as time returned to the usual speeds humans experienced it as it leapt from one present to the next.

Letje allowed the present to unfold, ensuring that her friends got their gift, their anger and hatred satiated.

Arcene's sword arced down evilly, slicing into the earth, gouging out a deep line. She frowned at her poor aim but pulled the sword up fast, turning, pig-tails flying as she moved at lightening speed. Artek stood transfixed, staring in horror as he watched red hair fall in front of his eyes. He put a hand up to his hair, touching his forehead, his skin turning almost translucent in shock at the realization that the locks falling to the floor really were his own. It was then that Letje truly knew the man was insane, more concerned about his appearance whilst madness reigned all around him.

Gamm got to his feet, crouching forward ready to take on Artek once more, beaten to it by Mother Superior who leapt onto Artek's back and sank her teeth as deep as they would go into the back of his neck. He hardly seemed to notice, until suddenly he came back to himself, howling dementedly at the affront to his personal appearance, clamping down with hard delight on his lapse of control over the minds around him. He bucked and shook wildly, finally reaching behind and flipping the gray-fleshed body of Mother Superior over his head, her body cracking as she slammed hard into the ground on her back, mouth stained red with blood and flesh.

Artek spun around, side-stepping Gamm's assault even as he lost his awareness of why he was charging, turning past then coming to a standstill in a daze.

Gamm's shirt practically melted off his body as blue light in spiral patterns began to shine through the material then sear it away in a blue/white pulse in time to the rhythm pulsing from the recovering Mother Superior now sat on the floor amid the mayhem.

Gamm's huge muscular frame shone brightly, patterns rippling across his broad chest, matching the beating of his heart, the rise and fall of his ribcage, getting brighter and drawing in energy from The Noise as he seemed to visibly expand, veins bulging, forearms knotted with muscles. He reached out fast and grabbed Artek by his hair, yanking him back hard, then lifting him off the ground like he was a rag doll. Gamm's eyes cleared and he snarled into the face of Artek before flinging him at the feet of Arcene, his gift to her, knowing that this was as it should be.

Arcene said, "Sit Leel," and the dog flashed her a quick look before obeying. Arcene turned to Letje.

Letje stepped forward, allowing her consciousness to expand, to encompass everything, to see into the Awoken mind of Artek Ligertwood and wrap her power around the delicate tendrils of invisible energy that were right now threading their way through The Noise, poised to shut down the memories of all of them, take away their reality and stuff them into a closed box of happy uncaring quietude. She tugged tight, turning his manipulation back on itself, making his own strength work against him, adding an image of her own to the struggling mind of the man just now getting to his feet while the others looked on.

What she showed him was simple: an image of how he looked from her vantage point. Clothes torn and dirty, hair ridiculous and his enemies all around him. She didn't stop there, she showed him his son, held tight by the terrified woman; showed Artek the future that lay ahead for the child, the place he would take in the rule that was one day to be his, how strong and powerful the boy would be, what would be his and how handsome he would be.

More, she showed him more. Letje couldn't stop, wouldn't stop, vast energies pouring through her into the mind of what she could now see was pitiful in comparison to her own. She showed him all that she knew would be achieved, of the distant future, the lineage that was not to be Artek's, for he would be forgotten, a mean-spirited ancestor that was to be wiped from the family tree and never spoken of again.

On and on it went, Letje pounding visions into the man's brain, making him watch as the future unfolded, a future that wouldn't contain him, showing him all that could have been his and was now taken away.

Then Letje took her real punishment and she presented Artek with what she had seen — something so terrible she hardly wished it on anyone, but it was not her decision to make, this was the reality for the energy that comprised the very fabric of Artek, this was a decision of The Void.

The terrible emptiness spoke to him through Letje; she let it.

She opened up the cracks in the nothingness, showed him his timeless wait of countless years, showed him the short pathetic lives he would live over and over again as The Void gave the pitiful life what it deserved for failing to live up to what it had been given, what it had been capable of. Over and over again it would happen, brief spells of life in countless forms, dying terrible deaths, living and dying in the dark as creatures without eyes or limbs, as tiny insects and strange things at the bottom of the ocean. As worms and slugs and ants and even as human beings, as alien creatures impossible to understand and as nothing more than terrible genetic experiments performed in strange places in strange lands in the far past and distant future.

She showed him it all, the punishment that was nothing to do with her, but his debt for squandering what was the most precious thing in the Universe: not just life but consciousness, self-awareness and the knowledge that his actions brought harm to others.

He was to be given his punishment on a cosmic scale, enduring if not for eternity then as close to it as could be understood by the minds of human beings. And maybe, just maybe, at some point there would be a chance, a glimmer of hope for salvation as he fought and clawed his way out of the primordial soup to strive to reach sentience one day and have another chance at doing something worthwhile with his life.

It was over.

Artek sank to his knees, already lost to the world, mind reeling at the punishment that was to be doled out by all that ever was, all that ever would be.

The Void wasn't cruel, but neither was it forgiving. It simply was.

Letje nodded to Arcene.

Arcene gripped her sword in two hands, trailing it along the ground, turning away from Artek before spinning fast, sword rising, cleaving the air before she lowered it once more and placed it on the ground.

Without looking at Artek she walked over to the woman holding her baby and gently took the child from her arms. She held him up high as he kicked out playfully then she gave him the first kiss she had ever given him and hugged him tight to her chest.

Artek stood up awkwardly, looking in horror at the ground as his hand went to his sticky head, screaming a silent *no* into The Void as he stared in disbelief at his scalp lying in sharp contrast to the green grass, the top of his head sliced clean off, his full head of hair mocking him as he fell face forward. The last thing he saw before he died was Leel grabbing the flesh and hair and throwing it into the air playfully before flinging it away disinterestedly then bounding over to see who the new addition to the family was that Arcene was talking to in hushed tones.

"Are you alright?" said Letje.

"Fine, absolutely fine," said Gamm. "You?"

"Better now. Much better." Letje couldn't help noticing just how muscular Gamm was, and brushed her long hair away from her eyes, the moment somewhat spoiled when a naked Mother Superior tugged at her leg and said, "That was a good punishment."

"Maybe, maybe not," said Letje. "But it's over now, the end of the journey."

"Oh, I don't know about that," said Gamm, smiling back at Letje. "I have a feeling it's only just beginning."

~~~

Marcus slowly emerged from the chair, eyes flashing colors dementedly.

He smiled, then went to make a cup of tea.

Happy Thoughts

Bird was happy.

Bird had a family, a true family: both human and his direct offspring.

Bird also had family that was a combination of both.

He soared high above The Commorancy, staring intently in approval at the ever-expanding numbers of his kind that filled the air, perched majestically on the myriad spires, rooftops, gargoyles and living Rooms that were now his family home.

Bird was once more amused by the games of man.

Why not? It wasn't as if they were going to outlast him and his lineage.

Were they?

Hope

Letje sat on the throne in The Room For Punishment — there hadn't been any choice in the matter, and besides, it was where Fasolt spent most of his time now so it was nice to see him again. The body of the man that had tried to interfere with the running of The Commorancy in what, Letje had to admit, was a rather ingenious way, lay dead below, ceremonial death robes stained red — a familiar sight over the last three thousand years, but for the last millennia there had only been a handful of people that had to be dealt with. It seemed that finally people were accepting that The Commorancy did nothing but good, and as the population expanded so did the number of those coming and going from the home of humanity's salvation.

Bird nuzzled at Letje's ear, perched on a thick mound of scar tissue that Letje had finally had to control via internal body chemistry to stop it from becoming too inconvenient to her daily life.

Fasolt sat below on the steps, hardly moving, spending most of his time lost in The Noise, his body almost ashen now, so long had it been since he'd seen the sunlight. He lived in the Room now, and had done for going on two thousand years. His hair meandered down the steps, across the floor, weaving between the death chairs, twitching and curling to avoid the blood or the body. He didn't speak much any more, the odd word every few centuries if he felt so inclined. It didn't matter; it was as things should be.

His dreadlocks were gray verging on white now, alive with energy that drew sustenance from The Noise and kept Fasolt's body functioning, but year by year he became less present, slowly seeping away, lost in worlds Letje couldn't even begin to imagine, playing in time and space, following the threads of the past, dancing down timelines to watch civilization play out in infinite futures that all happened somewhere, just not here.

The Marcus', thirteen of them now — they always seemed to find another one every few centuries — stood, sat, chatted or stared off into The Void, watching life through multiple viewpoints, each experiencing the world a little differently, happy to be together for a brief spell where they didn't have to cope with living a life of such complexity. There had been more, many more of them, but some couldn't take such a convoluted existence and chose to pass fully into The Void, others cut the connection and went to have their own adventures, never to be shared with the others, personal and private, almost like a normal person experienced life.

Other Marcus' gave up their human bodies and spread throughout the world, some as animals, others as insect collectives, the many parts making up the whole, others drifting off into space as nothing more than motes that could stand the ravages of space, finally lost to the others because of the vast distances, the connection finally severed, but knowledge shared that grew those that remained in ways impossible to tell through words.

More Marcus' lived beneath the ground, simple creatures with no thoughts, just happy to be a part of the ecosystem, unknowing that there was such a world all around them. Others were a part of Bird's family now, some sharing bodies with the creatures' initial inhabitants, others the sole occupiers, taking up residence as the life of Bird's ancestors faded into The Void. They soared above the convoluted rooftops of The Commorancy, watching over the millennia as buildings crumbled and others took their place.

Arcene was by Letje's side, fifteen years old for eternity, smiling as a woman who appeared to be in her mid thirties whispered something in her ear. The woman had hair as silver as Arcene's, as had each generation of grandchildren then great grandchildren, on and on over the centuries then the millennia, each eventually Awakening, helping the world to repopulate, spreading across the globe, hunting out the few survivors, taking husbands, wives, caring for children found alone. Doing things; ensuring humanity continued.

By Letje's left side was a young boy, Letje's seventeenth son, now of age and staring in wonder at the swirling patterns that danced with life across his chest and down his arms, his father by his side, an arm on his shoulder, Gamm as proud of the boy as he was when he had held his first child, a girl so beautiful he thought his heart would break.

Nestled on a red velvet cushion, munching contently on a lettuce leaf, heavy-lidded eyes half closed, was Constantine Alexander XXXII. One of the Marcus' shared occupancy with the tortoise, a constant through the centuries that saw so much else change.

Letje smiled.

She wondered what the next few millennia would bring; she was sure it would be worth hanging around to find out.

The End

Author's Note

Well, that's a wrap I am afraid to say. This series of books has a special place in my heart — I feel like I know the characters so well they are like family now.

What can I say? I hope you enjoyed reading as much as I have enjoyed writing The Commorancy.

And you never know, maybe some of your favorite characters will get a series all of their very own. It wouldn't surprise me; I miss them already.

Can you do me a favor and leave a review for The Commorancy books? It greatly helps in terms of increasing visibility, so a few words, especially for the first in the series, or as many as you wish, would be greatly appreciated.

Want more from the same world right now? Well, why not take a look at the INK Trilogy? It's a total change of pace: fast and furious, but some of it will seem familiar. It's based right after The Lethargy, focusing on The Ink and one man's battle for survival.

Drop me a line at al@alkline.co.uk if you want to say hi.

Stay jiggy

Al

Sign up for The Newsletter for deals and new release announcements at http://www.alkline.co.uk/

52483178R00166

Made in the USA
Charleston, SC
20 February 2016